Three Act Tragedy

Agatha Christie is known throughout the world as the Queen of Crime. Her books have sold over a billion copies in English with another billion in 100 foreign countries. She is the most widely published author of all time and in any language, outsold only by the Bible and Shakespeare. She is the author of 80 crime novels and short story collections, 19 plays, and six novels written under the name of Mary Westmacott.

Agatha Christie's first novel, *The Mysterious Affair at Styles*, was written towards the end of the First World War, in which she served as a VAD. In it she created Hercule Poirot, the little Belgian detective who was destined to become the most popular detective in crime fiction since Sherlock Holmes. It was eventually published by The Bodley Head in 1920.

In 1926, after averaging a book a year, Agatha Christie wrote her masterpiece. *The Murder of Roger Ackroyd* was the first of her books to be published by Collins and marked the beginning of an author-publisher relationship which lasted for 50 years and well over 70 books. *The Murder of Roger Ackroyd* was also the first of Agatha Christie's books to be dramatised – under the name *Alibi* – and to have a successful run in London's West End. *The Mousetrap*, her most famous play of all, opened in 1952 and is the longest-running play in history.

Agatha Christie was made a Dame in 1971. She died in 1976, since when a number of books have been published posthumously: the bestselling novel *Sleeping Murder* appeared later that year, followed by her autobiography and the short story collections *Miss Marple's Final Cases*, *Problem at Pollensa Bay* and *While the Light Lasts*. In 1998 *Black Coffee* was the first of her plays to be novelised by another author, Charles Osborne.

The Agatha Christie Collection

The Man In The Brown Suit
The Secret of Chimneys
The Seven Dials Mystery
The Mysterious Mr Quin
The Sittaford Mystery
The Hound of Death
The Listerdale Mystery
Why Didn't They Ask Evans?
Parker Pyne Investigates
Murder Is Easy
And Then There Were None
Death Comes as the End
Sparkling Cyanide
Crooked House
They Came to Baghdad
Destination Unknown
Spider's Web *
The Unexpected Guest *
Ordeal by Innocence
The Pale Horse
Endless Night
Passenger To Frankfurt

Poirot
The Mysterious Affair at Styles
The Murder on the Links
Poirot Investigates
The Murder of Roger Ackroyd
The Big Four
The Mystery of the Blue Train
Black Coffee *
Peril at End House
Lord Edgware Dies
Murder on the Orient Express
Three-Act Tragedy
Death in the Clouds
The ABC Murders
Murder in Mesopotamia
Cards on the Table
Murder in the Mews
Dumb Witness
Death on the Nile
Appointment With Death
Hercule Poirot's Christmas
Sad Cypress
One, Two, Buckle My Shoe
Evil Under the Sun
Five Little Pigs
The Hollow
The Labours of Hercules

* novelised by Charles Osborne

Taken at the Flood
Mrs McGinty's Dead
After the Funeral
Hickory Dickory Dock
Dead Man's Folly
Cat Among the Pigeons
The Adventure of the Christmas Pudding
The Clocks
Third Girl
Hallowe'en Party
Elephants Can Remember
Poirot's Early Cases
Curtain: Poirot's Last Case

Marple
The Murder at the Vicarage
The Thirteen Problems
The Body in the Library
The Moving Finger
A Murder is Announced
They Do It With Mirrors
A Pocket Full of Rye
The 4.50 from Paddington
The Mirror Crack'd from Side to Side
A Caribbean Mystery
At Bertram's Hotel
Nemesis
Sleeping Murder
Miss Marple's Final Cases

Tommy & Tuppence
The Secret Adversary
Partners in Crime
N or M?
By the Pricking of My Thumbs
Postern of Fate

Published as Mary Westmacott
Giant's Bread
Unfinished Portrait
Absent in the Spring
The Rose and the Yew Tree
A Daughter's a Daughter
The Burden

Memoirs
An Autobiography
Come, Tell Me How You Live

Play Collections
The Mousetrap and Selected Plays
Witness for the Prosecution and
    Selected Plays

Agatha Christie

Three Act Tragedy

HARPER

HARPER

An imprint of HarperCollins*Publishers*
77–85 Fulham Palace Road,
Hammersmith, London W6 8JB
www.harpercollins.co.uk

This *Agatha Christie Signature Edition* published 2002
10 9 8 7 6 5 4 3 2 1

First published in Great Britain by Collins 1935

ISBN-13: 978-0-00-729323-0

Typeset by Palimpsest Book Production Limited,
Grangemouth, Stirlingshire

Printed and bound in India by
Gopsons Papers Ltd., Noida 201301

Dedicated to
My Friends, Geoffrey and Violet Shipston

Contents

Third Act

Discovery

Directed by
Sir Charles Cartwright

Assistant Directors
Mr Satterthwaite
Miss Hermione Lytton Gore

Clothes by
Ambrosine Ltd

Illumination by
Hercule Poirot

First Act

Suspicion

Chapter 1
Crow's Nest

Mr Satterthwaite sat on the terrace of 'Crow's Nest' and watched his host, Sir Charles Cartwright, climbing up the path from the sea.

Crow's Nest was a modern bungalow of the better type. It had no half timbering, no gables, no excrescences dear to a third-class builder's heart. It was a plain white solid building – deceptive as to size, since it was a good deal bigger than it looked. It owed its name to its position, high up, overlooking the harbour of Loomouth. Indeed from one corner of the terrace, protected by a strong balustrade, there was a sheer drop to the sea below. By road Crow's Nest was a mile from the town. The road ran inland and then zigzagged high up above the sea. On foot it was accessible in seven minutes by the steep fisherman's path that Sir Charles Cartwright was ascending at this minute.

Agatha Christie

Sir Charles was a well-built, sunburnt man of middle age. He wore old grey flannel trousers and a white sweater. He had a slight rolling gait, and carried his hands half closed as he walked. Nine people out of ten would say, 'Retired Naval man – can't mistake the type.' The tenth, and more discerning, would have hesitated, puzzled by something indefinable that did not ring true. And then perhaps a picture would rise, unsought: the deck of a ship – but not a real ship – a ship curtailed by hanging curtains of thick rich material – a man, Charles Cartwright, standing on that deck, light that was not sunlight streaming down on him, the hands half clenched, the easy gait and a voice – the easy pleasant voice of an English sailor and gentleman, a great deal magnified in tone.

'No, sir,' Charles Cartwright was saying, 'I'm afraid I can't give you any answer to that question.'

And swish fell the heavy curtains, up sprang the lights, an orchestra plunged into the latest syncopated measure, girls with exaggerated bows in their hair said, 'Chocolates? Lemonade?' The first act of *The Call of the Sea,* with Charles Cartwright as Commander Vanstone, was over.

From his post of vantage, looking down, Mr Satterthwaite smiled.

A dried-up little pipkin of a man, Mr Satterthwaite,

a patron of art and the drama, a determined but pleasant snob, always included in the more important house-parties and social functions (the words 'and Mr Satterthwaite' appeared invariably at the tail of a list of guests). Withal a man of considerable intelligence and a very shrewd observer of people and things.

He murmured now, shaking his head, 'I wouldn't have thought it. No, really, I wouldn't have thought it.'

A step sounded on the terrace and he turned his head. The big grey-haired man who drew a chair forward and sat down had his profession clearly stamped on his keen, kindly, middle-aged face. 'Doctor' and 'Harley Street'. Sir Bartholomew Strange had succeeded in his profession. He was a well-known specialist in nervous disorders, and had recently received a knighthood in the Birthday Honours list.

He drew his chair forward beside that of Mr Satterthwaite and said:

'What wouldn't you have thought? Eh? Let's have it.'

With a smile Mr Satterthwaite drew attention to the figure below rapidly ascending the path.

'I shouldn't have thought Sir Charles would have remained contented so long in – er – exile.'

'By Jove, no more should I!' The other laughed,

throwing back his head. 'I've known Charles since he was a boy. We were at Oxford together. He's always been the same – a better actor in private life than on the stage! Charles is always acting. He can't help it – it's second nature to him. Charles doesn't go out of a room – he "makes an exit" – and he usually has to have a good line to make it on. All the same, he likes a change of part – none better. Two years ago he retired from the stage – said he wanted to live a simple country life, out of the world, and indulge his old fancy for the sea. He comes down here and builds this place. His idea of a simple country cottage. Three bathrooms and all the latest gadgets! I was like you, Satterthwaite, I didn't think it would last. After all, Charles is human – he needs his audience. Two or three retired captains, a bunch of old women and a parson – that's not much of a house to play to. I thought the "simple fellow, with his love of the sea," would run for six months. Then, frankly, I thought he'd tire of the part. I thought the next thing to fill the bill would be the weary man of the world at Monte Carlo, or possibly a laird in the Highlands – he's versatile, Charles is.'

The doctor stopped. It had been a long speech. His eyes were full of affection and amusement as he watched the unconscious man below. In a couple of minutes he would be with them.

'However,' Sir Bartholomew went on, 'it seems we were wrong. The attraction of the simple life holds.'

'A man who dramatises himself is sometimes mis-judged,' pointed out Mr Satterthwaite. 'One does not take his sincerities seriously.'

The doctor nodded.

'Yes,' he said thoughtfully. 'That's true.'

With a cheerful halloo Charles Cartwright ran up the steps on to the terrace.

'*Mirabelle* surpassed herself,' he said. 'You ought to have come, Satterthwaite.'

Mr Satterthwaite shook his head. He had suffered too often crossing the Channel to have any illusions about the strength of his stomach afloat. He had observed the *Mirabelle* from his bedroom window that morning. There had been a stiff sailing breeze and Mr Satterthwaite had thanked heaven devoutly for dry land.

Sir Charles went to the drawing-room window and called for drinks.

'You ought to have come, Tollie,' he said to his friend. 'Don't you spend half your life sitting in Harley Street telling your pateints how good life on the ocean wave would be for them?'

'The great merit of being a doctor,' said Sir Bartholomew, 'is that you are not obliged to follow your own advice.'

Agatha Christie

Sir Charles laughed. He was still unconsciously playing his part – the bluff breezy Naval man. He was an extraordinarily good-looking man, beautifully-proportioned, with a lean humorous face, and the touch of grey at his temples gave him a kind of added distinction. He looked what he was – a gentleman first and an actor second.

'Did you go alone?' asked the doctor.

'No,' Sir Charles turned to take his drink from a smart parlourmaid who was holding a tray. 'I had a "hand". The girl Egg, to be exact.'

There was something, some faint trace of self-consciousness in his voice which made Mr Satterthwaite look up sharply.

'Miss Lytton Gore? She knows something about sailing, doesn't she?'

Sir Charles laughed rather ruefully.

'She succeeds in making me feel a complete landlubber; but I'm coming on – thanks to her.'

Thoughts slipped quickly in and out of Mr Satterthwaite's mind.

'I wonder – Egg Lytton Gore – perhaps that's why he hasn't tired – the age – a dangerous age – it's always a young girl at that time of life . . .'

Sir Charles went on: 'The sea – there's nothing like it – sun and wind and sea – and a simple shanty to come home to.'

And he looked with pleasure at the white building behind him, equipped with three bathrooms, hot and cold water in all the bedrooms, the latest system of central heating, the newest electrical fittings and a staff of parlourmaid, housemaid, chef, and kitchenmaid. Sir Charles's interpretation of simple living was, perhaps, a trifle exaggerated.

A tall and exceedingly ugly woman issued from the house and bore down upon them.

'Good morning, Miss Milray.'

'Good morning, Sir Charles. Good morning' (a slight inclination of the head towards the other two). 'This is the menu for dinner. I don't know whether you would like it altered in any way?'

Sir Charles took it and murmured:

'Let's see. Melon Cantaloupe, Bortsch Soup, Fresh Mackerel, Grouse, Soufflé Surprise, Canapé Diane . . . No, I think that will do excellently, Miss Milray. Everyone is coming by the four-thirty train.'

'I have already given Holgate his orders. By the way, Sir Charles, if you will excuse me, it would be better if I dined with you tonight.'

Sir Charles looked startled, but said courteously:

'Delighted, I am sure, Miss Milray – but – er –'

Miss Milray proceeded calmly to explain.

'Otherwise, Sir Charles, it would make thirteen at table; and so many people are superstitious.'

19

From her tone it could be gathered that Miss Milray would have sat down thirteen to dinner every night of her life without the slightest qualm. She went on:

'I think everything is arranged. I have told Holgate the car is to fetch Lady Mary and the Babbingtons. Is that right?'

'Absolutely. Just what I was going to ask you to do.'

With a slightly superior smile on her rugged countenance, Miss Milray withdrew.

'That,' said Sir Charles reverently, 'is a very remarkable woman. I'm always afraid she'll come and brush my teeth for me.'

'Efficiency personified,' said Strange.

'She's been with me for six years,' said Sir Charles. 'First as my secretary in London, and here, I suppose, she's a kind of glorified housekeeper. Runs this place like clockwork. And now, if you please, she's going to leave.'

'Why?'

'She says' – Sir Charles rubbed his nose dubiously – 'she *says* she's got an invalid mother. Personally I don't believe it. That kind of woman never had a mother at all. Spontaneously generated from a dynamo. No, there's something else.'

'Quite probably,' said Sir Bartholomew, 'people have been talking.'

'Talking?' The actor stared. Talking – what about?'

'My dear Charles. You know what talking means.'

'You mean talking about her – and me? With that face? And at her age?'

'She's probably under fifty.'

'I suppose she is,' Sir Charles considered the matter. 'But seriously, Tollie, have you *noticed* her face? It's got two eyes, a nose and a mouth, but it's not what you would call a *face* – not a *female* face. The most scandal-loving old cat in the neighbourhood couldn't seriously connect sexual passion with a face like that.'

'You underrate the imagination of the British spinster.'

Sir Charles shook his head.

'I don't believe it. There's a kind of hideous respectability about Miss Milray that even a British spinster must recognize. She is virtue and respectability personified – and a damned useful woman. I always choose my secretaries plain as sin.'

'Wise man.'

Sir Charles remained deep in thought for some minutes. To distract him, Sir Bartholomew asked: 'Who's coming this afternoon?'

'Angie, for one.'

'Angela Sutcliffe? That's good.'

Mr Satterthwaite leaned forward interestedly, keen to know the composition of the house-party. Angela

Sutcliffe was a well-known actress, no longer young, but with a strong hold on the public and celebrated for her wit and charm. She was sometimes spoken of as Ellen Terry's successor.

'Then there are the Dacres.'

Again Mr Satterthwaite nodded to himself. Mrs Dacres was Ambrosine, Ltd, that successful dress-making establishment. You saw it on programmes – 'Miss Blank's dresses in the first act by Ambrosine Ltd, Brook Street.' Her husband, Captain Dacres, was a dark horse in his own racing parlance. He spent a lot of time on race courses – had ridden himself in the Grand National in years gone by. There had been some trouble – nobody knew exactly – though rumours had been spread about. There had been no inquiry – nothing overt, but somehow at mention of Freddie Dacres people's eyebrows went up a little.

'Then there's Anthony Astor, the playwright.'

'Of course,' said Mr Satterthwaite. 'She wrote *One-Way Traffic*. I saw it twice. It made a great hit.'

He rather enjoyed showing that he knew that Anthony Astor was a woman.

'That's right,' said Sir Charles. 'I forget what her real name is – Wills, I think. I've only met her once. I asked her to please Angela. That's the lot – of the house-party, I mean.'

'And the locals?' asked the doctor.

'Oh, the locals! Well, there are the Babbingtons – he's the parson, quite a good fellow, not too parsonical, and his wife's a really nice woman. Lectures me on gardening. They're coming – and Lady Mary and Egg. That's all. Oh, yes, there's a young fellow called Manders, he's a journalist, or something. Good-looking young fellow. That completes the party.'

Mr Satterthwaite was a man of methodical nature. He counted heads.

'Miss Sutcliffe, one, the Dacres, three, Anthony Astor, four, Lady Mary and her daughter, six, the parson and his wife, eight, the young fellow nine, ourselves twelve. Either you or Miss Milray must have counted wrong, Sir Charles.'

'It couldn't be Miss Milray,' said Sir Charles with assurance. 'That woman's never wrong. Let me see: Yes, by Jove, you're right. I *have* missed out one guest. He'd slipped my memory.'

He chuckled. 'Wouldn't be best pleased at that, either. The fellow is the most conceited little devil I ever met.'

Mr Satterthwaite's eyes twinkled. He had always been of the opinion that the vainest men in creation were actors. He did not exempt Sir Charles Cartwright. This instance of the pot calling the kettle black amused him.

'Who is the egoist?' he asked.

'Rum little beggar,' said Sir Charles. 'Rather a celebrated little beggar, though. You may have heard of
him. Hercule Poirot. He's a Belgian.'

'The detective,' said Mr Satterthwaite. 'I have met
him. Rather a remarkable personage.'

'He's a character,' said Sir Charles.

'I've never met him,' said Sir Bartholomew, 'but I've
heard a good deal about him. He retired some time ago,
though, didn't he? Probably most of what I've heard is
legend. Well, Charles, I hope we shan't have a crime
this weekend.'

'Why? Because we've got a detective in the house?
Rather putting the cart before the horse, aren't you,
Tollie?'

'Well, it's by way of being a theory of mine.'

'What is your theory, doctor?' asked Mr Satterthwaite.

'That events come to people – not people to events.
Why do some people have exciting lives and other
people dull ones? Because of their surroundings? Not
at all. One man may travel to the ends of the earth and
nothing will happen to him. There will be a massacre
a week before he arrives, and an earthquake the day
after he leaves, and the boat that he nearly took will
be shipwrecked. And another man may live at Balham
and travel to the City every day, and things will happen
to him. He will be mixed up with blackmailing gangs
and beautiful girls and motor bandits. There are people

with a tendency to shipwrecks – even if they go on a boat on an ornamental lake something will happen to it. In the same way men like your Hercule Poirot don't have to look for crime – it comes to them.'

'In that case,' said Mr Satterthwaite, 'perhaps it is as well that Miss Milray is joining us, and that we are not sitting down thirteen to dinner.'

'Well,' said Sir Charles handsomely, 'you can have your murder, Tollie, if you're so keen on it. I make only one stipulation – that I shan't be the corpse.'

And, laughing, the three men went into the house.

Chapter 2
Incident Before Dinner

The principal interest of Mr Satterthwaite's life was people.

He was on the whole more interested in women than men. For a manly man, Mr Satterthwaite knew far too much about women. There was a womanish strain in his character which lent him insight into the feminine mind. Women all his life had confided in him, but they had never taken him seriously. Sometimes he felt a little bitter about this. He was, he felt, always in the stalls watching the play, never on the stage taking part in the drama. But in truth the rôle of onlooker suited him very well.

This evening, sitting in the large room giving on to the terrace, cleverly decorated by a modern firm to resemble a ship's cabin *de luxe*, he was principally interested in the exact shade of hair dye attained by Cynthia Dacres. It was an entirely new tone –

straight from Paris, he suspected – a curious and rather pleasing effect of greenish bronze. What Mrs Dacres really looked like it was impossible to tell. She was a tall woman with a figure perfectly disciplined to the demands of the moment. Her neck and arms were her usual shade of summer tan for the country – whether naturally or artificially produced it was impossible to tell. The greenish bronze hair was set in a clever and novel style that only London's best hairdresser could achieve. Her plucked eyebrows, darkened lashes, exquisitely made-up face, and mouth lip-sticked to a curve that its naturally straight line did not possess, seemed all adjuncts to the perfection of her evening gown of a deep and unusual blue, cut very simply it seemed (though this was ludicrously far from the case) and of an unusual material – dull, but with hidden lights in it.

'That's a clever woman,' said Mr Satterthwaite, eyeing her with approval. 'I wonder what she's really like.'

But this time he meant in mind, not in body.

Her words came drawlingly, in the mode of the moment.

'My dear, it wasn't possible. I mean, things either are possible or they're not. This wasn't. It was simply penetrating.'

That was the new word just now – everything was 'penetrating'.

Sir Charles was vigorously shaking cocktails and talking to Angela Sutcliffe, a tall, grey-haired woman with a mischievous mouth and fine eyes.

Dacres was talking to Bartholomew Strange.

'Everyone knows what's wrong with old Ladisbourne. The whole stable knows.'

He spoke in a high clipped voice – a little red, foxy man with a short moustache and slightly shifty eyes.

Beside Mr Satterthwaite sat Miss Wills, whose play, *One-Way Traffic*, had been acclaimed as one of the most witty and daring seen in London for some years. Miss Wills was tall and thin, with a receding chin and very badly waved fair hair. She wore pince-nez, and was dressed in exceedingly limp green chiffon. Her voice was high and undistinguished.

'I went to the South of France,' she said. 'But, really, I didn't enjoy it very much. Not friendly at all. But of course it's useful to me in my work – to see all the goings-on, you know.'

Mr Satterthwaite thought: 'Poor soul. Cut off by success from her spiritual home – a boarding-house in Bournemouth. That's where she'd like to be.' He marvelled at the difference between written works and their authors. That cultivated 'man-of-the-world' tone that Anthony Astor imparted to his plays – what faintest spark of it could be perceived in Miss Wills? Then he noticed that the pale-blue eyes behind the pince-nez were singularly intelligent. They were turned on him now with an appraising look that slightly disconcerted him. It was as though Miss Wills were painstakingly learning him by heart.

Sir Charles was just pouring out the cocktails.

'Let me get you a cocktail,' said Mr Satterthwaite, springing up.

Miss Wills giggled.

'I don't mind if I do,' she said.

The door opened and Temple announced Lady Mary Lytton Gore and Mr and Mrs Babbington and Miss Lytton Gore.

Mr Satterthwaite supplied Miss Wills with her cocktail and then sidled into the neighbourhood of Lady Mary Lytton Gore. As has been stated before, he had a weakness for titles.

Also, apart from snobbishness, he liked a gentlewoman, and that Lady Mary most undeniably was.

Left as a widow very badly off with a child of three, she had come to Loomouth and taken a small cottage where she had lived with one devoted maid ever since. She was a tall thin woman, looking older than her fifty-five years. Her expression was sweet and rather timid. She adored her daughter, but was a little alarmed by her.

Hermione Lytton Gore, usually known for some obscure reason as Egg, bore little resemblance to her mother. She was of a more energetic type. She was not, Mr Satterthwaite decided, beautiful, but she was undeniably attractive. And the cause of that attraction, he thought, lay in her abounding vitality. She seemed twice as alive as anyone in that room. She had dark hair, and grey eyes and was of medium height. It was something in the way the hair curled crisply in her neck, in the straight glance of the grey eyes, in the curve of the cheek, in the infectious laugh that gave one that impression of riotous youth and vitality.

She stood talking to Oliver Manders, who had just arrived.

'I can't think why sailing bores you so much. You used to like it.'

'Egg – my dear. One grows up.'

He drawled the words, raising his eyebrows.

A handsome young fellow, twenty-five at a guess. Something, perhaps, a little sleek about his good looks. Something else – something – was it foreign? Something unEnglish about him.

Somebody else was watching Oliver Manders. A little man with an egg-shaped head and very foreign-looking moustaches. Mr Satterthwaite had recalled himself to M. Hercule Poirot's memory. The little man had been very affable. Mr Satterthwaite suspected him of deliberately exaggerating his foreign mannerisms. His small twinkly eyes seemed to say, 'You expect me to be the buffoon? To play the comedy for you? *Bien* – it shall be as you wish!'

But there was no twinkle now in Hercule Poirot's eyes. He looked grave and a little sad.

The Rev. Stephen Babbington, rector of Loomouth, came and joined Lady Mary and Mr Satterthwaite. He was a man of sixty odd, with kind faded eyes and a disarming diffident manner. He said to Mr Satterthwaite:

'We are very lucky to have Sir Charles living among us. He has been most kind – most generous. A very pleasant neighbour to have. Lady Mary agrees, I am sure.'

Lady Mary smiled.

'I like him very much. His success hasn't spoilt him. In many ways he is,' her smile deepened, 'a child still.'

The parlourmaid approached with the tray of cocktails as Mr Satterthwaite reflected how unendingly maternal women were. Being of the Victorian generation, he approved that trait.

'You can have a cocktail, Mums,' said Egg, flashing up to them, glass in hand. 'Just one.'

'Thank you, dear,' said Lady Mary meekly.

'I think,' said Mr Babbington, 'that my wife would allow me to have one.'

And he laughed a little gentle clerical laugh.

Mr Satterthwaite glanced over at Mrs Babbington, who was talking earnestly to Sir Charles on the subject of manure.

'She's got fine eyes,' he thought.

Mrs Babbington was a big untidy woman. She looked full of energy and likely to be free from petty mindedness. As Charles Cartwright had said – a nice woman.

'Tell me,' Lady Mary leaned forward. 'Who is the young woman you were talking to when we came in – the one in green?'

'That's the playwright – Anthony Astor.'

'What? That – that anaemic-looking young woman? Oh!' She caught herself up. 'How dreadful of me. But it was a surprise. She doesn't look – I mean she looks exactly like an inefficient nursery governess.'

It was such an apt description of Miss Wills' appearance that Mr Satterthwaite laughed. Mr Babbington was peering across the room with amiable short-sighted eyes. He took a sip of his cocktail and choked a little. He was unused to cocktails, thought Mr Satterthwaite amusedly – probably they represented modernity to his mind – but he didn't like them. Mr Babbington took another determined mouthful with a slightly wry face and said:

'Is it the lady over there? Oh dear –'

His hand went to his throat.

Egg Lytton Gore's voice rang out:

'Oliver – you slippery Shylock –'

'Of course,' thought Mr Satterthwaite, 'that's it – not foreign – Jew!'

What a handsome pair they made. Both so young and good-looking . . . and quarrelling, too – always a healthy sign . . .

He was distracted by a sound at his side. Mr Babbington had risen to his feet and was swaying to and fro. His face was convulsed.

It was Egg's clear voice that drew the attention of the room, though Lady Mary had risen and stretched out an anxious hand.

'Look,' said Egg's voice. 'Mr Babbington is ill.'

Sir Bartholomew Strange came forward hurriedly, supporting the stricken man and half lifting him to a couch at one side of the room. The others crowded round, anxious to help, but impotent . . .

Two minutes later Strange straightened himself and shook his head. He spoke bluntly, aware that it was no use to beat about the bush.

'I'm sorry,' he said. 'He's dead . . . .'

Chapter 3
Sir Charles Wonders

'Come in here a minute, Satterthwaite, will you?'

Sir Charles poked his head out of the door.

An hour and a half had passed. To confusion had succeeded peace. Lady Mary had led the weeping Mrs Babbington out of the room and had finally gone home with her to the vicarage. Miss Milray had been efficient with the telephone. The local doctor had arrived and taken charge. A simplified dinner had been served, and by mutual consent the house-party had retired to their rooms after it. Mr Satterthwaite had been making his own retreat when Sir Charles had called to him from the door of the Ship-room where the death had taken place.

Mr Satterthwaite passed in, repressing a slight shiver as he did so. He was old enough not to like the sight of death . . . For soon, perhaps, he himself . . . But why think of that?

Agatha Christie

'I'm good for another twenty years,' said Mr Satterthwaite robustly to himself.

The only other occupant of the Ship-room was Bartholomew Strange. He nodded approval at the sight of Mr Satterthwaite.

'Good man,' he said. 'We can do with Satterthwaite. He knows life.'

A little surprised, Mr Satterthwaite sat down in an armchair near the doctor. Sir Charles was pacing up and down. He had forgotten the semi-clenching of his hands and looked definitely less naval.

'Charles doesn't like it,' said Sir Bartholomew. 'Poor old Babbington's death, I mean.'

Mr Satterthwaite thought the sentiment ill expressed. Surely nobody could be expected to 'like' what had occurred. He realized that Strange had quite another meaning from the bald one the words conveyed.

'It was very distressing,' said Mr Satterthwaite, cautiously feeling his way. 'Very distressing indeed,' he added with a reminiscent shiver.

'H'm, yes, it was rather painful,' said the physician, the professional accent creeping for a moment into his voice.

Cartwright paused in his pacing.

'Ever see anyone die quite like that before, Tollie?'

'No,' said Sir Bartholomew thoughtfully. 'I can't say that I have.

'But,' he added in a moment or two, 'I haven't really seen as many deaths as you might suppose. A nerve specialist doesn't kill off many of his patients. He keeps 'em alive and makes his income out of them. MacDougal has seen far more deceases than I have, I don't doubt.'

Dr MacDougal was the principal doctor in Loomouth, whom Miss Milray had summoned.

'MacDougal didn't see this man die. He was dead when he arrived. There was only what we could tell him, what you could tell him. He said it was some kind of seizure, said Babbington was elderly, and his health was none too good. That doesn't satisfy me.'

'Probably didn't satisfy him,' grunted the other. 'But a doctor has to say something. Seizure is a good word – means nothing at all, but satisfies the lay mind. And, after all, Babbington *was* elderly, and his health *had* been giving him trouble lately; his wife told us so. There may have been some unsuspected weakness somewhere.'

'Was that a typical fit or seizure, or whatever you call it?'

'Typical of what?'

'Of any known disease?'

'If you'd ever studied medicine,' said Sir Bartholomew, 'you'd know that there is hardly any such thing as a typical case.'

'What, precisely, are you suggesting, Sir Charles?' asked Mr Satterthwaite.

Cartwright did not answer. He made a vague gesture with his hand. Strange gave a slight chuckle.

'Charles doesn't know himself,' he said. 'It's just his mind turning naturally to the dramatic possibilities.'

Sir Charles made a reproachful gesture. His face was absorbed – thoughtful. He shook his head slightly in an abstracted manner.

An elusive resemblance teased Mr Satterthwaite – then he got it. Aristide Duval, the head of the Secret Service, unravelling the tangled plot of 'Underground Wires'. In another minute he was sure. Sir Charles was limping unconsciously as he walked. Aristide Duval had been known as The Man With a Limp.

Sir Bartholomew continued to apply ruthless common sense to Sir Charles's unformulated suspicions.

'Yes, what do you suspect, Charles? Suicide? Murder? Who wants to murder a harmless old clergyman? It's fantastic. Suicide? Well, I suppose that is a point. One might perhaps imagine a reason for Babbington wanting to make away with himself –'

'What reason?'

Sir Bartholomew shook his head gently.

'How can we tell the secrets of the human mind? Just one suggestion – suppose that Babbington had been told he suffered from an incurable disease –

such as cancer. Something of that kind might supply a motive. He might wish to spare his wife the pain of watching his own long-drawn-out suffering. That's only a suggestion, of course. There's nothing on earth to make us think that Babbington did want to put an end to himself.'

'I wasn't thinking so much of suicide,' began Sir Charles.

Bartholomew Strange again gave his low chuckle.

'Exactly. You're not out for probability. You want sensation – new and untraceable poison in the cocktails.'

Sir Charles made an expressive grimace.

'I'm not so sure I do want that. Damn it all, Tollie, remember *I* mixed those cocktails.'

'Sudden attack of homicidal mania, eh? I suppose the symptoms are delayed in our case, but we'll all be dead before morning.'

'Damn it all, you joke, but –' Sir Charles broke off irritably.

'I'm not really joking,' said the physician.

His voice had altered. It was grave, and not unsympathetic.

'I'm not joking about poor old Babbington's death. I'm casting fun at your suggestions, Charles, because – well – because I don't want you, thoughtlessly, to do harm.'

'Harm?' demanded Sir Charles.

'Perhaps you understand what I'm driving at, Mr Satterthwaite?'

'I think, perhaps, I can guess,' said Mr Satterthwaite.

'Don't you see, Charles,' went on Sir Bartholomew, 'that those idle suspicions of yours might be definitely harmful? These things get about. A vague suggestion of foul play, totally unfounded, might cause serious trouble and pain to Mrs Babbington. I've known things of that kind happen once or twice. A sudden death – a few idle tongues wagging – rumours flying all round the place – rumours that go on growing – and *that no one can stop*. Damn it all, Charles, don't you see how cruel and unnecessary it would be? You're merely indulging your vivid imagination in a gallop over a wholly speculative course.'

A look of irresolution appeared on the actor's face.

'I hadn't thought of it like that,' he admitted.

'You're a thundering good chap, Charles, but you *do* let your imagination run away with you. Come now: do you seriously believe anyone, *anyone at all*, would want to murder that perfectly harmless old man?'

'I suppose not,' said Sir Charles. 'No, as you say, it's ridiculous. Sorry, Tollie, but it wasn't really a mere "stunt" on my part. I did genuinely have a "hunch" that something was wrong.'

Mr Satterthwaite gave a little cough.

'May I make a suggestion? Mr Babbington was taken ill a very few moments after entering the room and just after drinking his cocktail. Now, I did happen to notice he made a wry face when drinking. I imagined because he was unused to the taste. But supposing that Sir Bartholomew's tentative suggestion is correct – that Mr Babbington may for some reason have wished to commit suicide. That does strike me as just possible, whereas the suggestion of murder seems quite ridiculous.

'I feel that it is possible, though not probable, that Mr Babbington introduced something into that glass unseen by us.

'Now I see that nothing has yet been touched in this room. The cocktail glasses are exactly where they were. This is Mr Babbington's. I know, because I was sitting here talking to him. I suggest that Sir Bartholomew should get the glass analysed – that can be done quite quietly and without causing any "talk".'

Sir Bartholomew rose and picked up the glass.

'Right,' he said. 'I'll humour you so far, Charles, and I'll bet you ten pounds to one that there's nothing in it but honest-to-God gin and vermouth.'

'Done,' said Sir Charles.

Then he added with a rueful smile:

'You know, Tollie, *you* are partly responsible for my flights of fancy.'

41

Agatha Christie

'I?'

'Yes, with your talk of crime this morning. You said this man, Hercule Poirot, was a kind of stormy petrel, that where he went crimes followed. No sooner does he arrive than we have a suspiciously sudden death. Of course my thoughts fly to murder at once.'

'I wonder,' said Mr Satterthwaite, and stopped.

'Yes,' said Charles Cartwright. 'I'd thought of that. What do you think, Tollie? Could we ask him what he thinks of it all? Is it etiquette, I mean?'

'A nice point,' murmured Mr Satterthwaite.

'I know medical etiquette, but I'm hanged if I know anything about the etiquette of detection.'

'You can't ask a professional singer to sing,' murmured Mr Satterthwaite. 'Can one ask a professional detective to detect? Yes, a very nice point.'

'Just an opinion,' said Sir Charles.

There was a gentle tap on the door, and Hercule Poirot's face appeared, peering in with an apologetic expression.

'Come in, man,' cried Sir Charles, springing up. 'We were just talking of you.'

'I thought perhaps I might be intruding.'

'Not at all. Have a drink.'

'I thank you, no. I seldom drink the whisky. A glass of sirop, now –'

But sirop was not included in Sir Charles's conception

of drinkable fluids. Having settled his guest in a chair, the actor went straight to the point.

'I'm not going to beat about the bush,' he said. 'We were just talking of you, M. Poirot, and – and – of what happened tonight. Look here, do you think there's anything wrong about it?'

Poirot's eyebrows rose. He said:

'Wrong? How do you mean that – wrong?'

Bartholomew Strange said, 'My friend has got an idea into his head that old Babbington was murdered.'

'And you do not think so – eh?'

'We'd like to know what you think.'

Poirot said thoughtfully:

'He was taken ill, of course, very suddenly – very suddenly indeed.'

'Just so.'

Mr Satterthwaite explained the theory of suicide and his own suggestion of having a cocktail glass analysed.

Poirot nodded approval.

'That, at any rate, can do no harm. As a judge of human nature, it seems to me unlikely in the extreme that anyone could wish to do away with a charming and harmless old gentleman. Still less does the solution of suicide appeal to me. However, the cocktail glass will tell us one way or another.'

'And the result of the analysis, you think, will be – what?'

Poirot shrugged his shoulders.

'Me? I can only guess. You ask me to guess what will be the result of the analysis?'

'Yes –?'

'Then I guess that they will find only the remains of a very excellent dry Martini.' (He bowed to Sir Charles.) 'To poison a man in a cocktail, one of many handed round on a tray – well, it would be a technique very – very – difficult. And if that charming old clergyman wanted to commit suicide, I do not think he would do it at a party. That would show a very decided lack of consideration for others, and Mr Babbington struck me as a very considerate person.' He paused. 'That, since you ask me, is my opinion.'

There was a moment's silence. Then Sir Charles gave a deep sigh. He opened one of the windows and looked out.

'Wind's gone round a point,' he said.

The sailor had come back and the Secret Service detective had disappeared.

But to the observant Mr Satterthwaite it seemed as though Sir Charles hankered slightly after the part he was not, after all, to play.

Chapter 4
A Modern Elaine

'Yes, but what do you think, Mr Satterthwaite? Really *think*?'

Mr Satterthwaite looked this way and that. There was no escape. Egg Lytton Gore had got him securely cornered on the fishing quay. Merciless, these modern young women – and terrifyingly alive.

'Sir Charles has put this idea into your head,' he said.

'No, he hasn't. It was there already. It's been there from the beginning. It was so frightfully sudden.'

'He was an old man, and his health wasn't very good –'

Egg cut the recital short.

'That's all tripe. He had neuritis and a touch of rheumatoid arthritis. That doesn't make you fall down in a fit. He never had fits. He was the sort of gentle creaking gate that would have lived to be ninety. What did you think of the inquest?'

'It all seemed quite – er – normal.'

'What did you think of Dr MacDougal's evidence? Frightfully technical, and all that – close description of the organs – but didn't it strike you that behind all that bombardment of words he was hedging? What he said amounted to this: that there was nothing to show death had not arisen from natural causes. He didn't say it was the result of natural causes.'

'Aren't you splitting hairs a little, my dear?'

'The point is that *he* did – he was puzzled, but he had nothing to go upon, so he had to take refuge in medical caution. What did Sir Bartholomew Strange think?'

Mr Satterthwaite repeated some of the physician's dictums.

'Pooh-poohed it, did he?' said Egg thoughtfully. 'Of course, he's a cautious man – I suppose a Harley Street big bug has to be.'

'There was nothing in the cocktail glass but gin and vermouth,' Mr Satterthwaite reminded her.

'That seems to settle it. All the same, something that happened after the inquest made me wonder –'

'Something Sir Bartholomew said to you?'

Mr Satterthwaite began to feel a pleasant curiosity.

'Not to me – to Oliver. Oliver Manders – he was at dinner that night, but perhaps you don't remember him.'

'Yes, I remember him very well. Is he a great friend of yours?'

'Used to be. Now we scrap most of the time. He's gone into his uncle's office in the city, and he's getting – well, a bit oily, if you know what I mean. Always talks of chucking it and being a journalist – he writes rather well. But I don't think it's any more than talk now. He wants to get rich. I think everybody is rather disgusting about money, don't you, Mr Satterthwaite?'

Her youth came home to him then – the crude, arrogant childishness of her.

'My dear,' he said, 'so many people are disgusting about so many things.'

'Most people are swine, of course,' agreed Egg cheerfully. 'That's why I'm really cut up about old Mr Babbington. Because you see, he really was rather a pet. He prepared me for confirmation and all that, and though of course a lot of that business is all bunkum, he really was rather sweet about it. You see, Mr Satterthwaite, I really believe in Christianity – not like Mother does, with little books and early service, and things – but intelligently and as a matter of history. The Church is all clotted up with the Pauline tradition – in fact the Church is a mess – but Christianity itself is all right. That's why I can't be a communist like Oliver. In practice our beliefs would work out much the same, things in common and ownership by all, but the difference – well, I needn't go into that.

But the Babbingtons really *were* Christians; they didn't poke and pry and condemn, and they were never unkind about people or things. They were pets – and there was Robin . . .'

'Robin?'

'Their son . . . He was out in India and got killed . . . I – I had rather a pash on Robin . . .'

Egg blinked. Her gaze went out to sea . . .

Then her attention returned to Mr Satterthwaite and the present.

'So, you see, I feel rather strongly about this. Supposing it wasn't a natural death . . .'

'My dear child!'

'Well, it's damned odd! You must admit it's damned odd.'

'But surely you yourself have just practically admitted that the Babbingtons hadn't an enemy in the world.'

'That's what's so queer about it. I can't think of any conceivable motive . . .'

'Fantastic! There was nothing in the cocktail.'

'Perhaps someone jabbed him with a hypodermic.'

'Containing the arrow poison of the South American Indians,' suggested Mr Satterthwaite, gently ridiculing.

Egg grinned.

'That's it. The good old untraceable stuff. Oh, well, you're all very superior about it. Some day, perhaps, you'll find out we are right.'

'We?'

'Sir Charles and I.' She flushed slightly.

Mr Satterthwaite thought in the words and metre of his generation when *Quotations for All Occasions* was to be found in every bookcase.

'Of more than twice her years,
Seam'd with an ancient swordcut on the cheek,
And bruised and bronzed, she lifted up her eyes
And loved him, with that love which was her doom.'

He felt a little ashamed of himself for thinking in quotations – Tennyson, too, was very little thought of nowadays. Besides, though Sir Charles was bronzed, he was not scarred, and Egg Lytton Gore, though doubtless capable of a healthy passion, did not look at all likely to perish of love and drift about rivers on a barge. There was nothing of the lily maid of Astolat about her.

'Except,' thought Mr Satterthwaite, 'her youth . . .'

Girls were always attracted to middle-aged men with interesting pasts. Egg seemed to be no exception to this rule.

'Why hasn't he ever married?' she asked abruptly.

'Well . . .' Mr Satterthwaite paused. His own answer, put bluntly, would have been, 'Caution,' but he realized that such a word would be unacceptable to Egg Lytton Gore.

Sir Charles Cartwright had had plenty of affairs with women, actresses and others, but he had always managed to steer clear of matrimony. Egg was clearly seeking for a more romantic explanation.

'That girl who died of consumption – some actress, name began with an M – wasn't he supposed to be very fond of her?'

Mr Satterthwaite remembered the lady in question. Rumour had coupled Charles Cartwright's name with hers, but only very slightly, and Mr Satterthwaite did not for a moment believe that Sir Charles had remained unmarried in order to be faithful to her memory. He conveyed as much tactfully.

'I suppose he's had lots of affairs,' said Egg.

'Er – h'm – probably,' said Mr Satterthwaite, feeling Victorian.

'I like men to have affairs,' said Egg. 'It shows they're not queer or anything.'

Mr Satterthwaite's Victorianism suffered a further pang. He was at a loss for a reply. Egg did not notice his discomfiture. She went on musingly.

'You know, Sir Charles is really cleverer than you'd think. He poses a lot, of course, dramatises himself; but behind all that he's got brains. He's far better sailing a boat than you'd ever think, to hear him talk. You'd think, to listen to him, that it was all pose, but it isn't. It's the same about this business. You think it's all done for effect – that he wants to play the part of the great detective. All I say is: I think he'd play it rather well.'

'Possibly,' agreed Mr Satterthwaite.

The inflection of his voice showed his feelings clearly enough. Egg pounced on them and expressed them in words.

'But your view is that "Death of a Clergyman" isn't a thriller. It's merely "Regrettable Incident at a Dinner Party". Purely a social catastrophe. What did M. Poirot think? *He* ought to know.'

'M. Poirot advised us to wait for the analysis of the cocktail; but in his opinion everything was quite all right.'

'Oh, well,' said Egg, 'he's getting old. He's a back number.' Mr Satterthwaite winced. Egg went on, unconscious of brutality: 'Come home and have tea with Mother. She likes you. She said so.'

Delicately flattered, Mr Satterthwaite accepted the invitation.

On arrival Egg volunteered to ring up Sir Charles and explain the non-appearance of his guest.

Mr Satterthwaite sat down in the tiny sitting-room with its faded chintzes and its well-polished pieces of old furniture. It was a Victorian room, what Mr Satterthwaite called in his own mind a lady's room, and he approved of it.

His conversation with Lady Mary was agreeable,

nothing brilliant, but pleasantly chatty. They spoke of Sir Charles. Did Mr Satterthwaite know him well? Not intimately, Mr Satterthwaite said. He had a financial interest in one of Sir Charles's plays some years ago. They had been friends ever since.

'He has great charm,' said Lady Mary, smiling. 'I feel it as well as Egg. I suppose you've discovered that Egg is suffering badly from hero worship?'

Mr Satterthwaite wondered if, as a mother, Lady Mary was not made slightly uneasy by that hero worship. But it did not seem so.

'Egg sees so little of the world,' she said, sighing. 'We are so badly off. One of my cousins presented her and took her to a few things in town, but since then she has hardly been away from here, except for an occasional visit. Young people, I feel, should see plenty of people and places – especially people. Otherwise – well, propinquity is sometimes a dangerous thing.'

Mr Satterthwaite agreed, thinking of Sir Charles and the sailing, but that this was not what was in Lady Mary's mind, she showed a moment or two later.

'Sir Charles's coming has done a lot for Egg. It has widened her horizon. You see, there are very few young people down here – especially men. I've always been afraid that Egg might marry someone simply from being thrown with one person only and seeing no one else.'

Mr Satterthwaite had a quick intuition.

'Are you thinking of young Oliver Manders?'

Lady Mary blushed in ingenuous surprise.

'Oh, Mr Satterthwaite, I don't know how you knew! I *was* thinking of him. He and Egg were together a lot at one time, and I know I'm old-fashioned, but I don't like some of his ideas.'

'Youth must have its fling,' said Mr Satterthwaite.

Lady Mary shook her head.

'I've been so afraid – it's quite suitable, of course, I know all about him, and his uncle, who has recently taken him into his firm, is a very rich man; it's not that – it's silly of me – but –'

She shook her head, unable to express herself further.

Mr Satterthwaite felt curiously intimate. He said quietly and plainly:

'All the same, Lady Mary, you wouldn't like your girl to marry a man twice her own age.'

Her answer surprised him.

'It might be safer so. If you do that, at least you know where you are. At that age a man's follies and sins are definitely behind him; they are not – still to come . . .'

Before Mr Satterthwaite could say any more, Egg rejoined them.

'You've been a long time, darling,' said her mother.

'I was talking to Sir Charles, my sweet. He's all

alone in his glory.' She turned reproachfully to Mr Satterthwaite. 'You didn't tell me the house-party had flitted.'

'They went back yesterday – all but Sir Bartholomew Strange. He was staying till tomorrow, but he was recalled to London by an urgent telegram this morning. One of his patients was in a critical condition.'

'It's a pity,' said Egg. 'Because I meant to study the house-party. I might have got a clue.'

'A clue to what, darling?'

'Mr Satterthwaite knows. Oh, well, it doesn't matter. Oliver's still here. We'll rope him in. He's got brains when he likes.'

When Mr Satterthwaite arrived back at Crow's Nest he found his host sitting on the terrace overlooking the sea.

'Hullo, Satterthwaite. Been having tea with the Lytton Gores?'

'Yes. You don't mind?'

'Of course not. Egg telephoned . . . Odd sort of girl, Egg . . .'

'Attractive,' said Mr Satterthwaite.

'H'm, yes, I suppose she is.'

He got up and walked a few aimless steps.

'I wish to God,' he said suddenly and bitterly, 'that I'd never come to this cursed place.'

Chapter 5

Flight From A Lady

Mr Satterthwaite thought to himself: 'He's got it badly.'

He felt a sudden pity for his host. At the age of fifty-two, Charles Cartwright, the gay debonair breaker of hearts, had fallen in love. And, as he himself realized, his case was doomed to disappointment. Youth turns to youth.

'Girls don't wear their hearts on their sleeves,' thought Mr Satterthwaite. 'Egg makes a great parade of her feeling for Sir Charles. She wouldn't if it really meant anything. Young Manders is the one.'

Mr Satterthwaite was usually fairly shrewd in his assumptions.

Still, there was probably one factor that he did not take into account, because he was unaware of it himself. That was the enhanced value placed by age on youth. To Mr Satterthwaite, an elderly man, the fact that Egg might prefer a middle-aged man to a young one was frankly incredible. Youth was to him so much the most magical of all gifts.

He felt strengthened in his beliefs when Egg rang up after dinner and demanded permission to bring Oliver along and 'have a consultation'.

Certainly a handsome lad, with his dark, heavy-lidded eyes and easy grace of movement. He had, it seemed, permitted himself to be brought – a tribute to Egg's energy; but his general attitude was lazily sceptical.

'Can't you talk her out of it, sir?' he said to Sir Charles. 'It's this appallingly healthy bucolic life she leads that makes her so energetic. You know, Egg, you really are detestably hearty. And your tastes are childish – crime – sensation – and all that bunk.'

'You're a sceptic, Manders?'

'Well, sir, really. That dear old bleating fellow. It's fantastic to think of anything else but natural causes.'

'I expect you're right,' said Sir Charles.

Mr Satterthwaite glanced at him. What part was Charles Cartwright playing tonight. Not the ex-Naval man – not the international detective. No, some new and unfamiliar rôle.

It came as a shock to Mr Satterthwaite when he realized what that rôle was. Sir Charles was playing second fiddle. Second fiddle to Oliver Manders.

He sat back with his head in shadow watching those

two, Egg and Oliver, as they disputed – Egg hotly, Oliver languidly.

Sir Charles looked older than usual – old and tired. More than once Egg appealed to him – hotly and confidently – but his response was lacking.

It was eleven o'clock when they left. Sir Charles went out on the terrace with them and offered the loan of an electric torch to help them down the stony path.

But there was no need of a torch. It was a beautiful moonlit night. They set off together, their voices growing fainter as they descended.

Moonlight or no moonlight, Mr Satterthwaite was not going to risk a chill. He returned to the Shiproom. Sir Charles stayed out on the terrace a little while longer.

When he came in he latched the window behind him, and striding to a side table poured himself out a whisky and soda.

'Satterthwaite,' he said, 'I'm leaving here tomorrow for good.'

'What?' cried Mr Satterthwaite, astonished.

A kind of melancholy pleasure at the effect he had produced showed for a minute on Charles Cartwright's face.

'It's the Only Thing To Do,' he said, obviously speaking in capital letters. 'I shall sell this place. What it has meant to me no one will ever know.' His voice dropped, lingeringly . . . effectively.

After an evening of second fiddle, Sir Charles's egoism was taking its revenge. This was the great Renunciation Scene, so often played by him in sundry and divers dramas. Giving Up the Other Man's Wife, Renouncing the Girl he Loved.

There was a brave flippancy in his voice as he went on.

'Cut your losses – it's the only way . . . Youth to youth . . . They're made for each other, those two . . . I shall clear out . . .'

'Where to?' asked Mr Satterthwaite.

The actor made a careless gesture.

'Anywhere. What does it matter?' He added with a slight change of voice, 'Probably Monte Carlo.' And then, retrieving what his sensitive taste could not but feel to be a slight anticlimax, 'In the heart of the desert or the heart of the crowd – what does it matter? The inmost core of man is solitary – alone. I have always been – a lonely soul . . .'

It was clearly an exit line.

He nodded to Mr Satterthwaite and left the room.

Mr Satterthwaite got up and prepared to follow his host to bed.

'But it won't be the heart of a desert,' he thought to himself with a slight chuckle.

On the following morning Sir Charles begged Mr Satterthwaite to forgive him if he went up to town that day.

'Don't cut your visit short, my dear fellow. You were staying till tomorrow, and I know you're going on to the Harbertons at Tavistock. The car will take you there. What I feel is that, having come to my decision, I mustn't look back. No, I mustn't look back.'

Sir Charles squared his shoulders with manly resolution, wrung Mr Satterthwaite's hand with fervour and delivered him over to the capable Miss Milray.

Miss Milray seemed prepared to deal with the situation as she had dealt with any other. She expressed no surprise or emotion at Sir Charles's overnight decision. Nor could Mr Satterthwaite draw her out on the point. Neither sudden deaths nor sudden changes of plan could excite Miss Milray. She accepted whatever happened as a fact and proceeded to cope with it in an efficient way. She telephoned to the house agents, despatched wires abroad, and wrote busily on her type-writer. Mr Satterthwaite escaped from the depressing spectacle of so much efficiency by strolling down to the quay. He was walking aimlessly along when he was seized by the arm from behind, and turned to confront a white-faced girl.

'What's all this?' demanded Egg fiercely.

'All what?' parried Mr Satterthwaite.

'It's all over the place that Sir Charles is going away – that he's going to sell Crow's Nest.'

'Quite true.'

'He is going away?'

'He's gone.'

'Oh!' Egg relinquished his arm. She looked suddenly like a very small child who has been cruelly hurt.

Mr Satterthwaite did not know what to say.

'Where has he gone?'

'Abroad. To the South of France.'

'Oh!'

Still he did not know what to say. For clearly there was more than hero worship here . . .

Pitying her, he was turning over various consolatory words in his mind when she spoke again – and startled him.

'Which of those damned bitches is it?' asked Egg fiercely.

Mr Satterthwaite stared at her, his mouth fallen open in surprise. Egg took him by the arm again and shook him violently.

'You must know,' she cried. 'Which of them? The grey-haired one or the other?'

'My dear, I don't know what you're talking about.'

'You do. You must. Of course it's some woman. He liked me – I know he liked me. One of those women the other night must have seen it, too, and determined to get him away from me. I hate women. Lousy cats. Did you see her clothes – that one with the green hair? They made me gnash my teeth with envy. A woman who has clothes like that has a pull – you can't deny it. She's quite old and ugly as sin, really, but what does it matter. She makes everyone else look like a dowdy curate's wife. Is it her? Or is it the other one with the grey hair? She's amusing – you can see that. She's got masses of S.A. And he called her Angie. It can't be the one like a wilted cabbage. Is it the smart one or is it Angie?'

'My dear, you've got the most extraordinary ideas into your head. He – er – Charles Cartwright isn't the least interested in either of those women.'

'I don't believe you. They're interested in him, anyway . . .'

'No, no, no, you're making a mistake. This is all imagination.'

'Bitches,' said Egg. 'That's what they are!'

'You mustn't use that word, my dear.'

'I can think of a lot worse things to say than that.'

'Possibly, possibly, but pray don't do so. I can assure you that you are labouring under a misapprehension.'

'Then why has he gone away – like this?'

Mr Satterthwaite cleared his throat.

'I fancy he – er – thought it best.'

Egg stared at him piercingly.

Agatha Christie

'Do you mean – because of *me*?'

'Well – something of the kind, perhaps.'

'And so he's legged it. I suppose I did show my hand a bit plainly . . . Men do hate being chased, don't they? Mums is right, after all . . . You've no idea how sweet she is when she talks about men. Always in the third person – so Victorian and polite. "A man hates being run after; a girl should always let the man make the running." Don't you think it's a sweet expression – make the running? Sounds the opposite of what it means. Actually that's just what Charles has done – made the running. He's running away from me. He's afraid. And the devil of it is, I can't go after him. If I did I suppose he'd take a boat to the wilds of Africa or somewhere.'

'Hermione,' said Mr Satterthwaite, 'are you serious about Sir Charles?'

The girl flung him an impatient glance.

'Of course I am.'

'What about Oliver Manders?'

Egg dismissed Oliver Manders with an impatient whisk of the head. She was following out a train of thought of her own.

'Do you think I might write to him? Nothing alarming. Just chatty girlish stuff . . . you know, put him at his ease, so that he'd get over his scare?'

She frowned.

'What a fool I've been. Mums would have managed it much better. They knew how to do the trick, those Victorians. All blushing retreat. I've been all wrong about it. I actually thought he needed encouraging. He seemed – well, he seemed to need a bit of help. Tell me,' she turned abruptly on Mr Satterthwaite, 'did he see me do my kissing act with Oliver last night?'

'Not that I know of. When –?'

'All in the moonlight. As we were going down the path. I thought he was still looking from the terrace. I thought perhaps if he saw me and Oliver – well, I thought it might wake him up a bit. Because he did like me. I could swear he liked me.'

'Wasn't that a little hard on Oliver?'

Egg shook her head decisively.

'Not in the least. Oliver thinks it's an honour for any girl to be kissed by him. It was damned bad for his conceit, of course; but one can't think of everything. I wanted to ginger up Charles. He's been different lately – more standoffish.'

'My dear child,' said Mr Satterthwaite, 'I don't think you realize quite why Sir Charles went away so suddenly. He thought that you cared for Oliver. He went away to save himself further pain.'

Egg whisked round. She caught hold of Mr Satterthwaite by the shoulders and peered into his face.

'Is that true? Is that really true? The mutt! The boob! Oh –!'

She released Mr Satterthwaite suddenly and moved along beside him with a skipping motion.

'Then he'll come back,' she said. 'He'll come back. If he doesn't –'

'Well, if he doesn't?'

Egg laughed.

'I'll get him back somehow. You see if I don't.'

It seemed as though allowing for difference of language Egg and the lily maid of Astolat had much in common, but Mr Satterthwaite felt that Egg's methods would be more practical than those of Elaine, and that dying of a broken heart would form no part of them.

Second Act

Certainty

Chapter 1

Sir Charles Receives A Letter

Mr Satterthwaite had come over for the day to Monte Carlo. His round of house-parties was over, and the Riviera in September was rather a favourite haunt of his.

He was sitting in the gardens enjoying the sun and reading a two-days-old *Daily Mail*.

Suddenly a name caught his attention. *Strange. Death of Sir Bartholomew Strange.* He read the paragraph through:

We much regret having to announce the death of Sir Bartholomew Strange, the eminent nerve specialist. Sir Bartholomew was entertaining a party of friends at his house in Yorkshire. Sir Bartholomew appeared to be in perfect health and spirits, and his demise occurred quite suddenly at the end of dinner. He was chatting with his friends and drinking a glass of port when he had

a sudden seizure and died before medical aid could be
summoned. Sir Bartholomew will be deeply regretted.
He was . . .

Here followed a description of Sir Bartholomew's
career and work.

Mr Satterthwaite let the paper slip from his hand.
He was very disagreeably impressed. A vision of the
physician as he had seen him last flashed across his
mind – big, jocund, in the pink of condition. And
now – dead. Certain words detached themselves from
their context and floated about disagreeably in Mr
Satterthwaite's mind. 'Drinking a glass of port.' 'Sudden seizure . . . Died before medical aid could be
summoned . . .'

Port, not a cocktail, but otherwise curiously reminiscent of that death in Cornwall. Mr Satterthwaite
saw again the convulsed face of the mild old clergyman . . .

Supposing that after all . . .

He looked up to see Sir Charles Cartwright coming
towards him across the grass.

'Satterthwaite, by all that's wonderful! Just the man
I'd have chosen to see. Have you seen about poor old
Tollie?'

'I was just reading it now.'

Sir Charles dropped into a chair beside him. He was

immaculately got up in yachting costume. No more grey flannels and old sweaters. He was the sophisticated yachtsman of the South of France.

'Listen, Satterthwaite, Tollie was as sound as a bell. Never had anything wrong with him. Am I being a complete fanciful ass, or does this business remind you of – of –?'

'Of that business at Loomouth? Yes, it does. But of course we may be mistaken. The resemblance may be only superficial. After all, sudden deaths occur the whole time from a variety of causes.'

Sir Charles nodded his head impatiently. Then he said:

'I've just got a letter – from Egg Lytton Gore.'

Mr Satterthwaite concealed a smile.

'The first you've had from her?'

Sir Charles was unsuspecting.

'No. I had a letter soon after I got here. It followed me about a bit. Just giving me the news and all that. I didn't answer it . . . Dash it all, Satterthwaite, I didn't dare answer it . . . The girl had no idea, of course, but I didn't want to make a fool of myself.'

Mr Satterthwaite passed his hand over his mouth where the smile still lingered.

'And this one?' he asked.

'This is different. It's an appeal for help . . .'

'Help?' Mr Satterthwaite's eyebrows went up.

Agatha Christie

'She was there – you see – in the house – when it happened.'

'You mean she was staying with Sir Bartholomew Strange at the time of his death?'

'Yes.'

'What does she say about it?'

Sir Charles had taken a letter from his pocket. He hesitated for a moment, then he handed it to Mr Satterthwaite.

'You'd better read it for yourself.'

Mr Satterthwaite opened out the sheet with lively curiosity.

'Dear Sir Charles, – I don't know when this will get to you. I do hope soon. I'm so worried, I don't know what to do. You'll have seen, I expect, in the papers that Sir Bartholomew Strange is dead. Well, he died just the same way as Mr Babbington. It can't be a coincidence – it can't – it can't . . . I'm worried to death . . .

'Look here, can't you come home and do something? It sounds a bit crude put like that, but you did have suspicions before, and nobody would listen to you, and now it's your own friend who's been killed; and perhaps if you don't come back nobody will ever find out the truth, and I'm sure you could. I feel it in my bones . . .

'And there's something else. I'm worried, definitely,

about someone . . . He had absolutely nothing to do with it, I know that, but things might look a bit odd. Oh, I can't explain in a letter. But won't you come back? You could find out the truth. I know you could.

'Yours in haste,
'EGG.'

'Well?' demanded Sir Charles impatiently. 'A bit incoherent of course; she wrote it in a hurry. But what about it?'

Mr Satterthwaite folded the letter slowly to give himself a minute or two before replying.

He agreed that the letter was incoherent, but he did not think it had been written in a hurry. It was, in his view, a very careful production. It was designed to appeal to Sir Charles's vanity, to his chivalry, and to his sporting instincts.

From what Mr Satterthwaite knew of Sir Charles, that letter was a certain draw.

'Who do you think she means by "someone", and "he"?' he asked.

'Manders, I suppose.'

'Was he there, then?'

'Must have been. I don't know why. Tollie never met him except on that one occasion at my house. Why he should ask him to stay, I can't imagine.'

'Did he often have those big house-parties?'

71

Agatha Christie

'Three or four times a year. Always one for the St Leger.'

'Did he spend much time in Yorkshire?'

'Had a big sanatorium – nursing home, whatever you like to call it. He bought Melfort Abbey (it's an old place), restored it and built a sanatorium in the grounds.'

'I see.'

Mr Satterthwaite was silent for a minute or two. Then he said:

'I wonder who else there was in the house-party?'

Sir Charles suggested that it might be in one of the other newspapers, and they went off to institute a newspaper hunt.

'Here we are,' said Sir Charles.

He read aloud:

'Sir Bartholomew Strange is having his usual house-party for the St Leger. Amongst the guests are Lord and Lady Eden, Lady Mary Lytton Gore, Sir Jocelyn and Lady Campbell, Captain and Mrs Dacres, and Miss Angela Sutcliffe, the well-known actress.'

He and Mr Satterthwaite looked at each other.

'The Dacres and Angela Sutcliffe,' said Sir Charles. 'Nothing about Oliver Manders.'

'Let's get today's *Continental Daily Mail*,' said

72

Mr Satterthwaite. 'There might be something in that.'

Sir Charles glanced over the paper. Suddenly he stiffened.

'My God, Satterthwaite, listen to this:

'SIR BARTHOLOMEW STRANGE.

'At the inquest today on the late Sir Bartholomew Strange, a verdict of Death by Nicotine Poisoning was returned, there being no evidence to show how or by whom the poison was administered.'

He frowned.

'Nicotine poisoning. Sounds mild enough – not the sort of thing to make a man fall down in a fit. I don't understand all this.'

'What are you going to do?'

'Do? I'm going to book a berth on the Blue Train tonight.'

'Well,' said Mr Satterthwaite, 'I might as well do the same.'

'You?' Sir Charles wheeled round on him, surprised.

'This sort of thing is rather in my line,' said Mr Satterthwaite modestly. 'I've – er – had a little experience. Besides, I know the Chief Constable in that part of the world rather well – Colonel Johnson. That will come in useful.'

'Good man,' cried Sir Charles. 'Let's go round to the Wagon Lits offices.'

Mr Satterthwaite thought to himself:

'The girl's done it. She's got him back. She said she would. I wonder just exactly how much of her letter was genuine.'

Decidedly, Egg Lytton Gore was an opportunist.

When Sir Charles had gone off to the Wagon Lits offices, Mr Satterthwaite strolled slowly through the gardens. His mind was still pleasantly engaged with the problem of Egg Lytton Gore. He admired her resource and her driving power, and stifled that slightly Victorian side of his nature which disapproved of a member of the fairer sex taking the initiative in affairs of the heart.

Mr Satterthwaite was an observant man. In the midst of his cogitations on the female sex in general, and Egg Lytton Gore in particular, he was unable to resist saying to himself:

'Now where have I seen that particular shaped head before?'

The owner of the head was sitting on a seat gazing thoughtfully ahead of him. He was a little man whose moustaches were out of proportion to his size.

A discontented-looking English child was standing nearby, standing first on one foot, then the other, and occasionally meditatively kicking the lobelia edging.

'Don't do that, darling,' said her mother, who was absorbed in a fashion paper.

'I haven't anything to do,' said the child.

The little man turned his head to look at her, and Mr Satterthwaite recognized him.

'M. Poirot,' he said. 'This is a very pleasant surprise.'

M. Poirot rose and bowed.

'*Enchanté, monsieur.*'

They shook hands, and Mr Satterthwaite sat down.

'Everyone seems to be in Monte Carlo. Not half an hour ago I ran across Sir Charles Cartwright, and now you.'

'Sir Charles, he also is here?'

'He's been yachting. You know that he gave up his house at Loomouth?'

'Ah, no, I did not know it. I am surprised.'

'I don't know that I am. I don't think Cartwright is really the kind of man who likes to live permanently out of the world.'

'Ah, no, I agree with you there. I was surprised for another reason. It seemed to me that Sir Charles had a particular reason for staying in Loomouth – a very charming reason, eh? Am I not right? The little demoiselle who calls herself, so amusingly, the egg?'

His eyes were twinkling gently.

'Oh, so you noticed that?'

'Assuredly I noticed. I have the heart very susceptible

to lovers – you too, I think. And *la jeunesse*, it is always touching.'

He sighed.

'I think,' said Mr Satterthwaite, 'that actually you have hit on Sir Charles's reason for leaving Loomouth. He was running away.'

'From Mademoiselle Egg? But it is obvious that he adores her. Why, then, run?'

'Ah,' said Mr Satterthwaite, 'you don't understand our Anglo-Saxon complexes.'

M. Poirot was following his own line of reasoning.

'Of course,' he said, 'it is a good move to pursue. Run from a woman – immediately she follows. Doubtless Sir Charles, a man of much experience, knows that.'

Mr Satterthwaite was rather amused.

'I don't think it was quite that way,' he said. 'Tell me, what are you doing out here? A holiday?'

'My time is all holidays nowadays. I have succeeded. I am rich. I retire. Now I travel about seeing the world.'

'Splendid,' said Mr Satterthwaite.

'*N'est-ce pas?*'

'Mummy,' said the English child, 'isn't there anything to *do*?'

'Darling,' said her mother reproachfully, 'isn't it lovely to have come abroad and to be in the beautiful sunshine?'

'Yes, but there's nothing to do.'

'Run about – amuse yourself. Go and look at the sea.'

'*Maman*,' said a French child, suddenly appearing. '*Joue avec moi.*'

A French mother looked up from her book.

'*Amuse toi avec ta balle, Marcelle.*'

Obediently the French child bounced her ball with a gloomy face.

'*Je m'amuse*,' said Hercule Poirot; and there was a very curious expression on his face.

Then, as if in answer to something he read in Mr Satterthwaite's face, he said:

'But yet, you have the quick perceptions. It is as you think –'

He was silent for a minute or two, then he said:

'See you, as a boy I was poor. There were many of us. We had to get on in the world. I entered the Police Force. I worked hard. Slowly I rose in that Force. I began to make a name for myself. I made a name for myself. I began to acquire an international reputation. At last, I was due to retire. There came the War. I was injured. I came, a sad and weary refugee, to England. A kind lady gave me hospitality. She died – not naturally; no, she was killed. *Eh bien*, I set my wits to work. I employed my little grey cells. I discovered her murderer. I found that I was not yet finished. No, indeed, my powers were stronger than ever. Then began my second career, that of a private inquiry agent in England. I have solved many fascinating and baffling problems. Ah, monsieur, I have lived! The psychology of human nature, it is wonderful. I grew rich. Some day, I said to myself, I will have all the money I need. I will realize all my dreams.'

He laid a hand on Mr Satterthwaite's knee.

'My friend, *beware of the day when your dreams come true*. That child near us, doubtless she too has dreamt of coming abroad – of the excitement – of how different everything would be. You understand?'

'I understand,' said Mr Satterthwaite, 'that you are *not* amusing yourself.'

Poirot nodded.

'Exactly.'

There were moments when Mr Satterthwaite looked like Puck. This was one of them. His little wrinkled face twitched impishly. He hesitated. Should he? Should he not?

Slowly he unfolded the newspaper he was still carrying.

'Have you seen this, M. Poirot?'

With his forefinger he indicated the paragraph he meant.

The little Belgian took the paper. Mr Satterthwaite watched him as he read. No change came over his face, but the Englishman had the impression that his body stiffened, as does that of a terrier when it sniffs a rathole.

Hercule Poirot read the paragraph twice, then he folded the paper and returned it to Mr Satterthwaite.

'That is interesting,' he said.

'Yes. It looks, does it not, as though Sir Charles Cartwright had been right and we had been wrong.'

'Yes,' said Poirot. 'It seems as though we had been wrong . . . I will admit it, my friend, I could not believe that so harmless, so friendly an old man could have been murdered . . . Well, it may be that I was wrong . . . Although, see you, this other death may be coincidence. Coincidences do occur – the most amazing coincidences. I, Hercule Poirot, have known coincidences that would surprise you . . .'

He paused, and went on:

'Sir Charles Cartwright's instinct may have been right. He is an artist – sensitive – impressionable – he feels things, rather than reasons about them . . . Such a method in life is often disastrous – but it is sometimes justified. I wonder where Sir Charles is now.'

Mr Satterthwaite smiled.

'I can tell you that. He is in the office of the Wagon Lits Co. He and I are returning to England tonight.'

'Aha!' Poirot put immense meaning into the exclamation. His eyes, bright, inquiring, roguish, asked a question. 'What zeal he has, our Sir Charles. He is determined, then, to play this rôle, the rôle of the amateur policeman? Or is there another reason?'

Mr Satterthwaite did not reply, but from his silence Poirot seemed to deduce an answer.

'I see,' he said. 'The bright eyes of Mademoiselle are concerned in this. It is not only crime that calls?'

'She wrote to him,' said Mr Satterthwaite, 'begging him to return.'

Poirot nodded.

'I wonder now,' he said. 'I do not quite understand –'

Mr Satterthwaite interrupted.

'You do not understand the modern English girl? Well, that is not surprising. I do not always understand them myself. A girl like Miss Lytton Gore –'

In his turn Poirot interrupted.

'Pardon. You have misunderstood me. I understand Miss Lytton Gore very well. I have met such another – many such others. You call the type modern; but it is – how shall I say? – age-long.'

Mr Satterthwaite was slightly annoyed. He felt that he – and only he – understood Egg. This preposterous foreigner knew nothing about young English womanhood.

Poirot was still speaking. His tone was dreamy – brooding.

'A knowledge of human nature – what a dangerous thing it can be.'

'A useful thing,' corrected Mr Satterthwaite.

'Perhaps. It depends upon the point of view.'

'Well –' Mr Satterthwaite hesitated – got up. He was a little disappointed. He had cast the bait and the fish had not risen. He felt that his own knowledge of human nature was at fault. 'I will wish you a pleasant holiday.'

'I thank you.'

'I hope that when you are next in London you will come and see me.' He produced a card. 'This is my address.'

'You are most amiable, Mr Satterthwaite. I shall be charmed.'

'Goodbye for the present, then.'

'Goodbye, and *bon voyage.*'

Mr Satterthwaite moved away. Poirot looked after him for a moment or two, then once more he stared straight ahead of him, looking out over the blue Mediterranean.

So he sat for at least ten minutes.

The English child reappeared.

'I've looked at the sea, Mummy. What shall I do next?'

'An admirable question,' said Hercule Poirot under his breath.

He rose and walked slowly away – in the direction of the Wagon Lits offices.

Chapter 2

The Missing Butler

Sir Charles and Mr Satterthwaite were sitting in Colonel Johnson's study. The chief constable was a big red-faced man with a barrack-room voice and a hearty manner.

He had greeted Mr Satterthwaite with every sign of pleasure and was obviously delighted to make the acquaintance of the famous Charles Cartwright.

'My missus is a great playgoer. She's one of your – what do the Americans call it? – fans. That's it – fans. I like a good play myself – good clean stuff that is, some of the things they put on the stage nowadays – faugh!'

Sir Charles, conscious of rectitude in this respect – he had never put on 'daring' plays, responded suitably with all his easy charm of manner. When they came to mention the object of their visit Colonel Johnson was only too ready to tell them all he could.

'Friend of yours, you say? Too bad – too bad. Yes, he was very popular round here. That sanatorium of his is very highly spoken of, and by all accounts Sir Bartholomew was a first-rate fellow, as well as being at the top of his profession. Kind, generous, popular all round. Last man in the world you'd expect to be murdered – and murder is what it looks like. There's nothing to indicate suicide, and anything like accident seems out of the question.'

'Satterthwaite and I have just come back from abroad,' said Sir Charles. 'We've only seen snippets here and there in the papers.'

'And naturally you want to know all about it. Well, I'll tell you exactly how the matter stands. I think there's no doubt the butler's the man we've got to look for. He was a new man – Sir Bartholomew had only had him a fortnight, and the moment after the crime he disappears – vanishes into thin air. That looks a bit fishy, doesn't it? Eh, what?'

'You've no notion where he went?'

Colonel Johnson's naturally red face got a little redder.

'Negligence on our part, you think. I admit it damn' well looks like it. Naturally the fellow was under observation – just the same as everyone else. He answered our questions quite satisfactorily – gave the London agency which obtained him the place. Last employer, Sir Horace Bird. All very civil spoken, no signs of panic. Next thing was he'd gone – and the house under observation. I've hauled my men over the coals, but they swear they didn't bat an eyelid.'

'Very remarkable,' said Mr Satterthwaite.

'Apart from everything else,' said Sir Charles thoughtfully, 'it seems a damn' fool thing to do. As far as he knew, the man wasn't suspected. By bolting he draws attention to himself.'

'Exactly. And not a hope of escape. His description's been circulated. It's only a matter of days before he's pulled in.'

'Very odd,' said Sir Charles. 'I don't understand it.'

'Oh, the reason's clear enough. He lost his nerve. Got the wind up suddenly.'

'Wouldn't a man who had the nerve to commit murder have the nerve to sit still afterward?'

'Depends. Depends. I know criminals. Chicken-livered, most of them. He thought he was suspected, and he bolted.'

'Have you verified his own account of himself?'

'Naturally, Sir Charles. That's plain routine work. London Agency confirms his story. He had a written reference from Sir Horace Bird, recommending him warmly. Sir Horace himself is in East Africa.'

'So the reference might have been forged?'

'Exactly,' said Colonel Johnson, beaming upon Sir Charles, with the air of a schoolmaster congratulating a bright pupil. 'We've wired to Sir Horace, of course, but it may be some little time before we get a reply. He's on safari.'

'When did the man disappear?'

'Morning after the death. There was a doctor present at the dinner – Sir Jocelyn Campbell – bit of a toxicologist, I understand; he and Davis (local man) agreed over the case, and our people were called in immediately. We interviewed everybody that night. Ellis (that's the butler) went to his room as usual and was missing in the morning. His bed hadn't been slept in.'

'He slipped away under cover of the darkness?'

'Seems so. One of the ladies staying there, Miss Sutcliffe, the actress – you know her, perhaps?'

'Very well, indeed.'

'Miss Sutcliffe has made a suggestion to us. She suggested that the man had left the house through a secret passage.' He blew his nose apologetically. 'Sounds rather Edgar Wallace stuff, but it seems there was such a thing. Sir Bartholomew was rather proud of it. He showed it to Miss Sutcliffe. The end of it comes out among some fallen masonry about half a mile away.'

'That would be a possible explanation, certainly,'

agreed Sir Charles. 'Only – would the butler know of the existence of such a passage?'

'That's the point, of course. My missus always says servants know everything. Daresay she's right.'

'I understand the poison was nicotine,' said Mr Satterthwaite.

'That's right. Most unusual stuff to use, I believe. Comparatively rare. I understand if a man's a heavy smoker, such as the doctor was, it would tend to complicate matters. I mean, he might have died of nicotine poisoning in a natural way. Only, of course, this business was too sudden for that.'

'How was it administered?'

'We don't know,' admitted Colonel Johnson. 'That's going to be the weak part of the case. According to medical evidence, it could only have been swallowed a few minutes previous to death.'

'They were drinking port, I understand?'

'Exactly. Seems as though the stuff was in the port; but it wasn't. We analysed his glass. That glass had contained port, and nothing but port. The other wine glasses had been cleared, of course, but they were all on a tray in the pantry, unwashed, and not one of them contained anything it shouldn't. As for what he ate, it was the same as everybody else had. Soup, grilled sole, pheasant and chipped potatoes, chocolate soufflé, soft roes on toast. His cook's been with him fifteen years.

Agatha Christie

No, there doesn't seem to be any way he could have been given the stuff, and yet there it is in the stomach. It's a nasty problem.'

Sir Charles wheeled round on Mr Satterthwaite.

'The same thing,' he said excitedly. 'Exactly the same as before.'

He turned apologetically to the chief constable.

'I must explain. A death occurred at my house in Cornwall –'

Colonel Johnson looked interested.

'I think I've heard about that. From a young lady – Miss Lytton Gore.'

'Yes, she was there. She told you about it?'

'She did. She was very set on her theory. But, you know, Sir Charles, I can't believe there's anything in that theory. It doesn't explain the flight of the butler. Your man didn't disappear by any chance?'

'Haven't got a man – only a parlourmaid.'

'She couldn't have been a man in disguise?'

Thinking of the smart and obviously feminine Temple, Sir Charles smiled.

Colonel Johnson also smiled apologetically.

'Just an idea,' he said. 'No, I can't say I put much reliance in Miss Lytton Gore's theory. I understand the death in question was an elderly clergyman. Who would want to put an old clergyman out of the way?'

'That's just the puzzling part of it,' said Sir Charles.

'I think you'll find it's just coincidence. Depend on it, the butler's our man. Very likely he's a regular criminal. Unluckily we can't find any of his fingerprints. We had a fingerprint expert go over his bedroom and the butler's pantry, but he had no luck.'

'If it was the butler, what motive can you suggest?'

'That, of course, is one of our difficulties,' admitted Colonel Johnson. 'The man might have been there with intent to steal, and Sir Bartholomew might have caught him out.'

'Both Sir Charles and Mr Satterthwaite remained courteously silent. Colonel Johnson himself seemed to feel that the suggestion lacked plausibility.

'The fact of the matter is, one can only theorize. Once we've got John Ellis under lock and key and have found out who he is, and whether he's ever been through our hands before – well, the motive may be as clear as day.'

'You've been through Sir Bartholomew's papers, I suppose?'

'Naturally, Sir Charles. We've given that side of the case every attention. I must introduce you to Superintendent Crossfield, who has charge of the case. A most reliable man. I pointed out to him, and he was quick to agree with me, that Sir Bartholomew's profession might have had something to do with the crime. A doctor knows many professional secrets. Sir Bartholomew's papers were all neatly filed and docketed – his secretary, Miss Lyndon, went through them with Crossfield.'

'And there was nothing?'

'Nothing at all suggestive, Sir Charles.'

'Was anything missing from the house – silver, jewellery, anything like that?'

'Nothing whatsoever.'

'Who exactly was staying in the house?'

'I've got a list – now where is it? Ah, I think Crossfield has it. You must meet Crossfield; as a matter of fact, I'm expecting him any minute now to report' – as a bell went – 'that's probably the man now.'

Superintendent Crossfield was a large, solid-looking man, rather slow of speech, but with a fairly keen blue eye.

He saluted his superior officer, and was introduced to the two visitors.

It is possible that had Mr Satterthwaite been alone he would have found it hard to make Crossfield unbend. Crossfield didn't hold with gentlemen from London – amateurs coming down with 'ideas'. Sir Charles, however, was a different matter. Superintendent Crossfield had a childish reverence for the glamour of the stage. He had twice seen Sir Charles act, and the excitement and rapture of seeing this hero of the footlights in a flesh-and-blood manner made him as friendly and loquacious as could be wished.

'I saw you in London, sir, I did. I was up with the wife. *Lord Aintree's Dilemma* – that's what the play was. In the pit, I was – and the house was crowded out – we had to stand two hours beforehand. But nothing else would do for the wife. "I must see Sir Charles Cartwright in *Lord Aintree's Dilemma*," she said. At the Pall Mall Theatre, it was.'

'Well,' said Sir Charles, 'I've retired from the stage now, as you know. But they still know my name at the Pall Mall.' He took out a card and wrote a few words on it. 'You give this to the people at the box office next time you and Mrs Crossfield are having a jaunt to town, and they'll give you a couple of the best seats going.'

'I take that very kindly of you, Sir Charles – very kindly, indeed. My wife will be all worked up when I tell her about this.'

After this Superintendent Crossfield was as wax in the ex-actor's hands.

'It's an odd case, sir. Never come across a case of nicotine poisoning before in all my experience. No more has our Doctor Davis.'

'I always thought it was a kind of disease you got from over-smoking.'

'To tell the truth, so did I, sir. But the doctor says that the pure alkaloid is an odourless liquid, and that a few drops of it are enough to kill a man almost instantaneously.'

Sir Charles whistled.

'Potent stuff.'

'As you say, sir. And yet it's in common use, as you might say. Solutions are used to spray roses with. And of course it can be extracted from ordinary tobacco.'

'Roses,' said Sir Charles. 'Now, where have I heard –?'

He frowned, then shook his head.

'Anything fresh to report, Crossfield?' asked Colonel Johnson.

'Nothing definite, sir. We've had reports that our man Ellis has been seen at Durham, at Ipswich, at Balham, at Land's End, and a dozen other places. That's all got to be sifted out for what it's worth.' He turned to the other two. 'The moment a man's description is circulated as wanted, he's seen by someone all over England.'

'What is the man's description?' asked Sir Charles.

Johnson took up a paper.

'John Ellis, medium height, say five-foot seven, stoops slightly, grey hair, small side whiskers, dark eyes, husky voice, tooth missing in upper jaw, visible when he smiles, no special marks or characteristics.'

'H'm,' said Sir Charles. 'Very nondescript, bar the side whiskers and the tooth, and the first will be off by now, and you can't rely on his smiling.'

'The trouble is,' said Crossfield, 'that nobody observes anything. The difficulty I had in getting anything but the vaguest description out of the maids at the Abbey. It's always the same. I've had descriptions of one and the same man, and he's been called tall, thin, short, stout, medium height, thickset, slender – not one in fifty really uses their eyes properly.'

'You're satisfied in your own mind, Superintendent, that Ellis is the man? . . .'

'Why else did he bolt, sir? You can't get away from that.'

'That's the stumbling block,' said Sir Charles thoughtfully.

Crossfield turned to Colonel Johnson and reported the measures that were being taken. The Colonel nodded approval and then asked the Superintendent for the list of inmates of the Abbey on the night of the crime. This was handed to the two new inquirers. It ran as follows:

MARTHA LECKIE, cook.
BEATRICE CHURCH, upper-housemaid.
DORIS COKER, under-housemaid.
VICTORIA BALL, between-maid.
ALICE WEST, parlourmaid.
VIOLET BASSINGTON, kitchenmaid.
(Above have all been in service of deceased for some time

*and bear good character. Mrs Leckie has been there for
fifteen years.)*

*GLADYS LYNDON – secretary, thirty-three, has been
secretary to Sir Bartholomew Strange for three years, can
give no information as to likely motive.*

Guests:

LORD AND LADY EDEN, 187 Cadogan Square.

*SIR JOCELYN and LADY CAMPBELL, 1256
Harley Street.*

*MISS ANGELA SUTCLIFFE, 28 Cantrell Mansions,
S.W.3.*

*CAPTAIN and MRS DACRES, 3 St John's House,
W.1. (Mrs Dacres carries on business as Ambrosine, Ltd,
Brook Street.)*

*LADY MARY and MISS HERMIONE LYTTON
GORE, Rose Cottage, Loomouth.*

*MISS MURIEL WILLS, 5 Upper Cathcart Road,
Tooting.*

*MR OLIVER MANDERS, Messrs Speier & Ross, Old
Broad Street, E.C.2.*

'H'm,' said Sir Charles. 'The Tooting touch was
omitted by the papers. I see young Manders was
there, too.'

'That's by way of being an accident, sir,' said Superintendent Crossfield. 'The young gentleman ran his car
into a wall just by the Abbey, and Sir Bartholomew,

who I understood was slightly acquainted with him, asked him to stay the night.'

'Careless thing to do,' said Sir Charles cheerfully.

'It was that, sir,' said the Superintendent. 'In fact, I fancy myself the young gentleman must have had one over the eight, as the saying goes. What made him ram the wall just where he did I can't imagine, if he was sober at the time.'

'Just high spirits, I expect,' said Sir Charles.

'Spirits it was, in my opinion, sir.'

'Well, thank you very much, Superintendent. Any objection to our going and having a look at the Abbey, Colonel Johnson?'

'Of course not, my dear sir. Though I'm afraid you won't learn much more there than I can tell you.'

'Anybody there?'

'Only the domestic staff, sir,' said Crossfield. 'The house-party left immediately after the inquest, and Miss Lyndon has returned to Harley Street.'

'We might, perhaps, see Dr – er – Davis, too?' suggested Mr Satterthwaite.

'Good idea.'

They obtained the doctor's address, and having thanked Colonel Johnson warmly for his kindness, they left.

Chapter 3
Which Of Them?

As they walked along the street, Sir Charles said:

'Any ideas, Satterthwaite?'

'What about you?' asked Mr Satterthwaite. He liked
to reserve judgment until the last possible moment.

Not so Sir Charles. He spoke emphatically:

'They're wrong, Satterthwaite. They're all wrong.
They've got the butler on the brain. The butler's done
a bunk – ergo, the butler's the murderer. It doesn't fit.
No, it doesn't fit. You can't leave that other death out
of account – the one down at my place.'

'You're still of the opinion that the two are connected?'

Mr Satterthwaite asked the question, though he had
already answered it in the affirmative in his own mind.

'Man, they *must* be connected. Everything points to
it . . . We've got to find the common factor – someone
who was present on both occasions –'

'Yes,' said Mr Satterthwaite. 'And that's not going to be as simple a matter as one might think, on the face of it. We've got too many common factors. Do you realize, Cartwright, that practically every person who was present at the dinner at your house was present here?'

Sir Charles nodded.

'Of course I've realized that – but do you realize what deduction one can draw from it?'

'I don't quite follow you, Cartwright?'

'Dash it all, man, do you suppose that's coincidence? No, it was *meant*. Why are all the people who were at the first death present at the second? Accident? Not on your life. It was plan – design – Tollie's plan.'

'Oh!' said Mr Satterthwaite. 'Yes, it's possible . . .'

'It's certain. You didn't know Tollie as well as I did, Satterthwaite. He was a man who kept his own counsel, and a very patient man. In all the years I've known him I've never known Tollie give utterance to a rash opinion or judgment.

'Look at it this way: Babbington's murdered – yes, *murdered* – I'm not going to hedge, or mince terms – murdered one evening in my house. Tollie ridicules me gently for my suspicions in the matter, but all the time he's got suspicions of his own. He doesn't talk about them – that's not his way. But quietly, in his own mind, he's building up a case. I don't know what he had to build upon. It can't, I think, be a case against any one particular person. He believed that one of those people was responsible for the crime, and he made a plan, a test of some kind to find out which person it was.'

'What about the other guests, the Edens and the Campbells?'

'Camouflage. It made the whole thing less obvious.'

'What do you think the plan was?'

'Sir Charles shrugged his shoulders – an exaggerated foreign gesture. He was Aristide Duval, that master mind of the Secret Service. His left foot limped as he walked.

'How can we know? I am not a magician. I cannot guess. But there *was* a plan . . . It went wrong, because the murderer was just one degree cleverer than Tollie thought . . . He struck first . . .'

'He?'

'Or she. Poison is as much a woman's weapon as a man's – more so.'

Mr Satterthwaite was silent. Sir Charles said:

'Come now, don't you agree? Or are you on the side of public opinion? *"The butler's the man. He done it."*'

'What's your explanation of the butler?'

'I haven't thought about him. In my view he doesn't matter . . . I could suggest an explanation.'

'Such as?'

'Well, say that the police are right so far – Ellis is a

professional criminal, working in, shall we say, with a gang of burglars. Ellis obtains this post with false credentials. Then Tollie is murdered. What is Ellis's position? A man is killed, and in the house is a man whose fingerprints are at Scotland Yard, and who is known to the police. Naturally he gets the wind up and bolts.'

'By the secret passage?'

'Secret passage be damned. He dodged out of the house while one of the fat-headed constables who were watching the house was taking forty winks.'

'It certainly seems more probable.'

'Well, Satterthwaite, what's your view?'

'Mine?' said Mr Satterthwaite. 'Oh, it's the same as yours. It has been all along. The butler seems to me a very clumsy red herring. I believe that Sir Bartholomew and poor old Babbington were killed by the same person.'

'One of the house-party?'

'One of the house-party.'

There was silence for a minute or two, and then Mr Satterthwaite asked casually:

'Which of them do you think it was?'

'My God, Satterthwaite, how can I tell?'

'You can't tell, of course,' said Mr Satterthwaite mildly. 'I just thought you might have some idea – you know, nothing scientific or reasoned. Just an ordinary guess.'

'Well, I haven't . . .' He thought for a minute and then burst out: 'You know, Satterthwaite, the moment you begin to *think* it seems impossible that any of them did it.'

'I suppose your theory is right,' mused Mr Satterthwaite. 'As to the assembling of the suspects, I mean. We've got to take it into account that there were certain definite exclusions. Yourself and myself and Mrs Babbington, for instance. Young Manders, too, he was out of it.'

'Manders?'

'Yes, his arrival on the scene was an accident. He wasn't asked or expected. That lets him out of the circle of suspects.'

'The dramatist woman, too – Anthony Astor.'

'No, no, she was there. Miss Muriel Wills of Tooting.'

'So she was – I'd forgotten the woman's name was Wills.'

He frowned. Mr Satterthwaite was fairly good at reading people's thoughts. He estimated with fair accuracy what was passing through the actor's mind. When the other spoke, Mr Satterthwaite mentally patted himself on the back.

'You know, Satterthwaite, you're right. I don't think it was definitely suspected people that he asked – because, after all, Lady Mary and Egg were there . . . No, he wanted to stage some reproduction of the first business, perhaps . . . He suspected someone, but he wanted other eye-witnesses there to confirm matters. Something of that kind . . .'

'Something of the kind,' agreed Mr Satterthwaite. 'One can only generalize at this stage. Very well, the Lytton Gores are out of it, you and I and Mrs Babbington and Oliver Manders are out of it. Who is left? Angela Sutcliffe?'

'Angie? My dear fellow. She's been a friend of Tollie's for years.'

'Then it boils down to the Dacres . . . In fact, Cartwright, you suspect the Dacres. You might just as well have said so when I asked you.'

Sir Charles looked at him. Mr Satterthwaite had a mildly triumphant air.

'I suppose,' said Cartwright slowly, 'that I do. At least, I don't suspect them . . . They just seem rather more possible than anyone else. I don't know them very well, for one thing. But for the life of me, I can't see why Freddie Dacres, who spends his life on the racecourse, or Cynthia, who spends her time designing fabulously expensive clothes for women, should have any desire to remove a dear, insignificant old clergyman . . .'

He shook his head, then his face brightened.

'There's the Wills woman. I forgot her again. What is there about her that continually makes you forget her? She's the most damnably nondescript creature I've ever seen.'

Mr Satterthwaite smiled.

'I rather fancy she might embody Burns's famous line – "A chiel's amang ye takin' notes." I rather fancy that Miss Wills spends her time taking notes. There are sharp eyes behind that pair of glasses. I think you'll find that anything worth noticing in this affair has been noticed by Miss Wills.'

'Do you?' said Sir Charles doubtfully.

'The next thing to do,' said Mr Satterthwaite, 'is to have some lunch. After that, we'll go out to the Abbey and see what we can discover on the spot.'

'You seem to be taking very kindly to this, Satterthwaite,' said Sir Charles, with a twinkle of amusement.

'The investigation of crime is not new to me,' said Mr Satterthwaite. 'Once when my car broke down and I was staying at a lonely inn –'

He got no further.

'I remember,' said Sir Charles, in his high, clear carrying actor's voice, 'when I was touring in 1921 . . .'

Sir Charles won.

Chapter 4

The Evidence Of The Servants

Nothing could have been more peaceful than the grounds and building of Melfort Abbey as the two men saw it that afternoon in the September sunshine. Portions of the Abbey were fifteenth century. It had been restored and a new wing added on to it. The new Sanatorium was out of sight of the house, with grounds of its own.

Sir Charles and Mr Satterthwaite were received by Mrs Leckie, the cook, a portly lady, decorously gowned in black, who was tearful and voluble. Sir Charles she already knew, and it was to him she addressed most of her conversation.

'You'll understand, I'm sure, sir, what it's meant to me. The master's death and all. Policemen all over the place, poking their noses here and there – would you believe it, even the dusbins they had to have their noses in, and questions! – they wouldn't have done

with asking questions. Oh, that I should have lived to
see such a thing – the doctor, such a quiet gentleman as
he always was, and made Sir Bartholomew, too, which
a proud day it was to all of us, as Beatrice and I well
remember, though she's been here two years less than
I have. And such questions as that police fellow (for
gentleman I will not call him, having been accustomed
to gentlemen and their ways and knowing what's what),
fellow, I say, whether or not he is a superintendent –'
Mrs Leckie paused, took breath and extricated herself
from the somewhat complicated conversational morass
into which she had fallen. 'Questions, that's what I say,
about all the maids in the house, and good girls they
are, every one of them – not that I'd say that Doris
gets up when she should do in the morning. I have to
speak about it at least once a week, and Vickie, she's
inclined to be impertinent, but, there, with the young
ones you can't expect the training – their mothers don't
give it to them nowadays – but good girls they are, and
no police superintendent shall make me say otherwise.
"Yes," I said to him, "you needn't think I'm going to
say anything against my girls. They're good girls, they
are, and as to having anything to do with murder, why
it's right-down wicked to suggest such a thing."'

Mrs Leckie paused.

'Mr Ellis, now – that's different. I don't know anything about Mr Ellis, and couldn't answer for him in

any way, he having been brought from London, and strange to the place, while Mr Baker was on holiday.'

'Baker?' asked Mr Satterthwaite.

'Mr Baker had been Sir Bartholomew's butler for the last seven years, sir. He was in London most of the time, in Harley Street. You'll remember him, sir?' She appealed to Sir Charles, who nodded. 'Sir Bartholomew used to bring him up here when he had a party. But he hadn't been so well in his health, so Sir Bartholomew said, and he gave him a couple of months' holiday, paid for him, too, in a place near the sea down near Brighton – a real kind gentleman the doctor was – and he took Mr Ellis on temporary for the time being, and so, as I said to that superintendent, I can't say anything about Mr Ellis, though, from all he said himself, he seems to have been with the best families, and he certainly had a gentlemanly way with him.'

'You didn't find anything – unusual about him?' asked Sir Charles hopefully.

'Well, it's odd your saying that, sir, because, if you know what I mean, I did and I didn't.'

'Sir Charles looked encouraging, and Mrs Leckie went on:

'I couldn't exactly say what it was, sir, but there was *some*thing –'

There always is – after the event – thought Mr

Satterthwaite to himself grimly. However much Mrs Leckie had despised the police, she was not proof against suggestion. If Ellis turned out to be the criminal, well, Mrs Leckie would have noticed *something*.

'For one thing, he was standoffish. Oh, quite polite, quite the gentleman – as I said, he'd been used to good houses. But he kept himself to himself, spent a lot of time in his own room; and he was – well, I don't know how to describe it, I'm sure – he was, well, there was *something –*'

'You didn't suspect he wasn't – not really a butler?' suggested Mr Satterthwaite.

'Oh, he'd been in service, right enough, sir. The things he knew – and about well-known people in society, too.'

'Such as?' suggested Sir Charles gently.

But Mrs Leckie became vague, and non-committal. She was not going to retail servants' hall gossip. Such a thing would have offended her sense of fitness.

To put her at her ease, Mr Satterthwaite said:

'Perhaps you can describe his appearance.'

Mrs Leckie brightened.

'Yes, indeed, sir. He was a very respectable-looking man – side-whiskers and grey hair, stooped a little, and he was growing stout – it worried him, that did. He had a rather shaky hand, too, but not from the cause you might imagine. He was a most abstemious man – not like many I've known. His eyes were a bit weak, I think, sir, the light hurt them – especially a bright light, used to make them water something cruel. Out with us he wore glasses, but not when he was on duty.'

'No special distinguishing marks?' asked Sir Charles. 'No scars? Or broken fingers? Or birth marks?'

'Oh, no, sir, nothing of that kind.'

'How superior detective stories are to life,' sighed Sir Charles. 'In fiction there is always some distinguishing characteristic.'

'He had a tooth missing,' said Mr Satterthwaite.

'I believe so, sir; I never noticed it myself.'

'What was his manner on the night of the tragedy?' asked Mr Satterthwaite in a slightly bookish manner.

'Well, really, sir, I couldn't say. I was busy, you see, in my kitchen. I hadn't time for noticing things.'

'No, no, quite so.'

'When the news came out that the master was dead we were struck all of a heap. I cried and couldn't stop, and so did Beatrice. The young ones, of course, were excited like, though very upset. Mr Ellis naturally wasn't so upset as we were, he being new, but he behaved very considerate, and insisted on Beatrice and me taking a little glass of port to counteract the shock. And to think that all the time it was he – the villain –'

Words failed Mrs Leckie, her eyes shone with indignation.

'He disappeared that night, I understand?'

'Yes, sir, went to his room like the rest of us, and in the morning he wasn't there. That's what set the police on him, of course.'

'Yes, yes, very foolish of him. Have you any idea how he left the house?'

'Not the slightest. It seems the police were watching the house all night, and they never saw him go – but, there, that's what the police are, human like anyone else, in spite of the airs they give themselves, coming into a gentleman's house and nosing round.'

'I hear there's some question of a secret passage,' Sir Charles said.

Mrs Leckie sniffed.

'That's what the police say.'

'Is there such a thing?'

'I've heard mention of it,' Mrs Leckie agreed cautiously.

'Do you know where it starts from?'

'No, I don't, sir. Secret passages are all very well, but they're not things to be encouraged in the servants' hall. It gives the girls ideas. They might think of slipping out that way. My girls go out by the back door and in by the back door, and then we know where we are.'

'Splendid, Mrs Leckie. I think you're very wise.'

Mrs Leckie bridled in the sun of Sir Charles's approval.

'I wonder,' he went on, 'if we might just ask a few questions of the other servants?'

'Of course, sir; but they can't tell you anything more than I can.'

'Oh, I know. I didn't mean so much about Ellis as about Sir Bartholomew himself – his manner that night, and so on. You see, he was a friend of mine.'

'I know, sir. I quite understand. There's Beatrice, and there's Alice. She waited at table, of course.'

'Yes, I'd like to see Alice.'

Mrs Leckie, however, had a belief in seniority. Beatrice Church, the upper-housemaid, was the first to appear.

She was a tall thin woman, with a pinched mouth, who looked aggressively respectable.

After a few unimportant questions, Sir Charles led the talk to the behaviour of the house-party on the fatal evening. Had they all been terribly upset? What had they said or done?

A little animation entered into Beatrice's manner. She had the usual ghoulish relish for tragedy.

'Miss Sutcliffe, she quite broke down. A very warm-hearted lady, she's stayed here before. I suggested bringing her a little drop of brandy, or a nice cup of tea, but she wouldn't hear of it. She took some aspirin, though. Said she was sure she couldn't sleep. But she was sleeping like a little child the next morning when I brought her her early tea.'

'And Mrs Dacres?'

'I don't think anything would upset that lady much.'

From Beatrice's tone, she had not liked Cynthia Dacres.

'Just anxious to get away, she was. Said her business would suffer. She's a big dressmaker in London, so Mr Ellis told us.'

A big dressmaker, to Beatrice, meant 'trade', and trade she looked down upon.

'And her husband?'

Beatrice sniffed.

'Steadied his nerves with brandy, he did. Or unsteadied them, some would say.'

'What about Lady Mary Lytton Gore?'

'A very nice lady,' said Beatrice, her tone softening. 'My great aunt was in service with her father at the Castle. A pretty young girl she was, so I've always heard. Poor she may be, but you can see she's someone – and so considerate, never giving trouble and always speaking so pleasant. Her daughter's a nice young lady, too. They didn't know Sir Bartholomew well, of course, but they were very distressed.'

'Miss Wills?'

Some of Beatrice's rigidity returned.

'I'm sure I couldn't say, sir, what Miss Wills thought about it.'

'Or what you thought about her?' asked Sir Charles. 'Come now, Beatrice, be human.'

An unexpected smile dinted Beatrice's wooden cheeks. There was something appealingly schoolboyish in Sir Charles's manner. She was not proof against the charm that nightly audiences had felt so strongly.

'Really, sir, I don't know what you want me to say.'

'Just what you thought and felt about Miss Wills.'

'Nothing, sir, nothing at all. She wasn't, of course –' Beatrice hesitated.

'Go on, Beatrice.'

'Well, she wasn't quite the "class" of the others, sir. She couldn't help it, I know,' went on Beatrice kindly. 'But she did things a real lady wouldn't have done. She pried, if you know what I mean, sir, poked and pried about.'

Sir Charles tried hard to get this statement amplified, but Beatrice remained vague. Miss Wills had poked and pried, but asked to produce a special instance of the poking, Beatrice seemed unable to do so. She merely repeated that Miss Wills pried into things that were no business of hers.

They gave it up at last, and Mr Satterthwaite said:

'Young Mr Manders arrived unexpectedly, didn't he?'

'Yes, sir, he had an accident with his car – just by the lodge gates, it was. He said it was a bit of luck its happening just here. The house was full, of course, but Miss Lyndon had a bed made up for him in the little study.'

'Was everyone very surprised to see him?'

'Oh, yes, sir, naturally, sir.'

Asked her opinion of Ellis, Beatrice was non-committal. She'd seen very little of him. Going off the way he did looked bad, though why he should want to harm the master she couldn't imagine. Nobody could.

'What was he like, the doctor, I mean? Did he seem to be looking forward to the house-party? Had he anything on his mind?'

'He seemed particularly cheerful, sir. Smiled to himself, he did, as though he had some joke on. I even heard him make a joke with Mr Ellis, a thing he'd never done with Mr Baker. He was usually a bit brusque with the servants, kind always, but not speaking to them much.'

'What did he say?' asked Mr Satterthwaite eagerly.

'Well, I forget exactly now, sir. Mr Ellis had come up with a telephone message, and Sir Bartholomew asked him if he was sure he'd got the names right, and Mr Ellis said quite sure – speaking respectful, of course. And the doctor he laughed and said, "You're a good fellow, Ellis, a first-class butler. Eh, Beatrice, what do you think?" And I was so surprised, sir, at the master speaking like that – quite unlike his usual self – that I didn't know what to say.'

'And Ellis?'

'He looked kind of disapproving, sir, as though it was the kind of thing he hadn't been used to. Stiff like.'

'What was the telephone message?' asked Sir Charles.

'The message, sir? Oh, it was from the Sanatorium – about a patient who had arrived there and had stood the journey well.'

'Do you remember the name?'

'It was a queer name, sir.' Beatrice hesitated. 'Mrs de Rushbridger – something like that.'

'Ah, yes,' said Sir Charles soothingly. 'Not an easy name to get right on the telephone. Well, thank you very much, Beatrice. Perhaps we could see Alice now.'

When Beatrice had left the room Sir Charles and Mr Satterthwaite compared notes by an interchange of glances.

'Miss Wills poked and pried, Captain Dacres got drunk, Mrs Dacres displayed no emotion. Anything there? Precious little.'

'Very little indeed,' agreed Mr Satterthwaite.

'Let's pin our hopes on Alice.'

Alice was a demure, dark-eyed young woman of thirty. She was only too pleased to talk.

She herself didn't believe Mr Ellis had anything to

do with it. He was too much the gentleman. The police had suggested he was just a common crook. Alice was sure he was nothing of the sort.

'You're quite certain he was an ordinary honest-to-God butler?' asked Sir Charles.

'Not ordinary, sir. He wasn't like any butler I've ever worked with before. He arranged the work different.'

'But you don't think he poisoned your master.'

'Oh, sir, I don't see how he could have done. I was waiting at table with him, and he couldn't have put anything in the master's food without my seeing him.'

'And the drink?'

'He went round with the wine, sir. Sherry first, with the soup, and then hock and claret. But what could he have done, sir? If there'd been anything in the wine he'd have poisoned everybody – or all those who took it. It's not as though the master had anything that nobody else had. The same thing with the port. All the gentlemen had port, and some of the ladies.'

'The wine glasses were taken out on a tray?'

'Yes, sir, I held the tray and Mr Ellis put the glasses on it, and I carried the tray out to the pantry, and there they were, sir, when the police came to examine them. The port glasses were still on the table. And the police didn't find anything.'

'You're quite sure that the doctor didn't have anything to eat or drink at dinner that nobody else had?'

'Not that I saw, sir. In fact, I'm sure he didn't.'

'Nothing that one of the guests gave him –'

'Oh, no, sir.'

'Do you know anything about a secret passage, Alice?'

'One of the gardeners told me something about it. Comes out in the wood where there's some old walls and things tumbled down. But I've never seen any opening to it in the house.'

'Ellis never said anything about it?'

'Oh, no, sir, he wouldn't know anything about it, I'm sure.'

'Who do you really think killed your master, Alice?'

'I don't know, sir. I can't believe anyone did . . . I feel it must have been some kind of accident.'

'H'm. Thank you, Alice.'

'If it wasn't for the death of Babbington,' said Sir Charles as the girl left the room, 'we could make her the criminal. She's a good-looking girl . . . And she waited at table . . . No, it won't do. Babbington was murdered; and anyway Tollie never noticed good-looking girls. He wasn't made that way.'

'But he was fifty-five,' said Mr Satterthwaite thoughtfully.

'Why do you say that?'

'It's the age a man loses his head badly about a girl – even if he hasn't done so before.'

Agatha Christie

'Dash it all, Satterthwaite, *I'm* – er – getting on for fifty-five.'

'I know,' said Satterthwaite.

And before his gentle twinkling gaze Sir Charles's eyes fell.

Unmistakably he blushed . . .

Chapter 5
In The Butler's Room

'How about an examination of Ellis's room?' asked Mr Satterthwaite, having enjoyed the spectacle of Sir Charles's blush to the full.

The actor seized at the diversion.

'Excellent, excellent. Just what I was about to suggest myself.'

'Of course the police have already searched it thoroughly.'

'The police –'

Aristide Duval waved the police away scornfully. Anxious to forget his momentary discomfiture, he flung himself with renewed vigour into his part.

'The police are blockheads,' he said sweepingly. 'What have they looked for in Ellis's room? Evidences of his guilt. We shall look for evidences of his innocence – an entirely different thing.'

'You're completely convinced of Ellis's innocence?'

'If we're right about Babbington, he *must* be innocent.'

'Yes, besides –'

Mr Satterthwaite did not finish his sentence. He had been about to say that if Ellis was a professional criminal who had been detected by Sir Bartholomew and had murdered him in consequence the whole affair would become unbearably dull. Just in time he remembered that Sir Bartholomew had been a friend of Sir Charles Cartwright's and was duly appalled by the callousness of the sentiments he had nearly revealed.

At first sight Ellis's room did not seem to offer much promise of discovery. The clothes in the drawers and hanging in the cupboard were all neatly arranged. They were well cut, and bore different tailors' marks. Clearly cast-offs given him in different situations. The underclothing was on the same scale. The boots were neatly polished and arranged on trees.

Mr Satterthwaite picked up a boot and murmured, 'Nines, just so, nines.' But, since there were no footprints in the case, that didn't seem to lead anywhere.

It seemed clear from its absence that Ellis had departed in his butler's kit, and Mr Satterthwaite pointed out to Sir Charles that that seemed rather a remarkable fact.

'Any man in his senses would have changed into an ordinary suit.'

'Yes, it's odd that . . . Looks almost, though that's

absurd, as if he *hadn't* gone at all . . . Nonsense, of course.'

They continued their search. No letters, no papers, except a cutting from a newspaper regarding a cure for corns, and a paragraph relating to the approaching marriage of a duke's daughter.

There was a small blotting-book and a penny bottle of ink on a side table – no pen. Sir Charles held up the blotting-book to the mirror, but without result. One page of it was very much used – a meaningless jumble, and the ink looked to both men old.

'Either he hasn't written any letters since he was here, or he hasn't blotted them,' deduced Mr Satterthwaite. 'This is an old blotter. Ah, yes –' With some gratification he pointed to a barely decipherable 'L. Baker' amidst the jumble.

'I should say Ellis hadn't used this at all.'

'That's rather odd, isn't it?' said Sir Charles slowly.

'What do you mean?'

'Well, a man usually writes letters . . .'

'Not if he's a criminal.'

'No, perhaps you're right . . . There must have been something fishy about him to make him bolt as he did . . . All we say is that he didn't murder Tollie.'

They hunted round the floor, raising the carpet, looking under the bed. There was nothing anywhere, except a splash of ink beside the fireplace. The room was disappointingly bare.

They left it in a somewhat disconcerted fashion. Their zeal as detectives was momentarily damped.

Possibly the thought passed through their minds that things were arranged better in books.

They had a few words with the other members of the staff, scared-looking juniors in awe of Mrs Leckie and Beatrice Church, but they elicited nothing further.

Finally they took their leave.

'Well, Satterthwaite,' said Sir Charles as they strolled across the park (Mr Satterthwaite's car had been instructed to pick them up at the lodge) 'anything strike you – anything at all?'

Mr Satterthwaite thought. He was not to be hurried into an answer – especially as he felt something *ought* to have struck him. To confess that the whole expedition had been a waste of time was an unwelcome idea. He passed over in his mind the evidence of one servant after another – the information was extraordinarily meagre.

As Sir Charles had summed it up just now, Miss Wills had poked and pried, Miss Sutcliffe had been very upset, Mrs Dacres had not been upset at all, and Captain Dacres had got drunk. Very little there, unless Freddie Dacres's indulgence showed the deadening of a guilty conscience. But Freddie Dacres, Mr Satterthwaite knew, quite frequently got drunk.

'Well?' repeated Sir Charles impatiently.

'Nothing,' confessed Mr Satterthwaite reluctantly. 'Except – well, I think we are entitled to assume from the clipping we found that Ellis suffered from corns.'

Sir Charles gave a wry smile.

'That seems quite a reasonable deduction. Does it – er – get us anywhere?'

Mr Satterthwaite confessed that it did not.

'The only other thing—' he said and then stopped.

'Yes? Go on, man. Anything may help.'

'It struck me as a little odd the way that Sir Bartholomew chaffed his butler – you know what the housemaid told us. It seems somehow uncharacteristic.'

'It *was* uncharacteristic,' said Sir Charles with emphasis. 'I knew Tollie well – better than you did – and I can tell you that he wasn't a facetious sort of man. He'd never have spoken like that unless – well, unless for some reason he wasn't quite normal at the time. You're right, Satterthwaite, that is a point. Now where does it get us?'

'Well,' began Mr Satterthwaite; but it was clear that Sir Charles's question had been merely a rhetorical one. He was anxious, not to hear Mr Satterthwaite's views, but to air his own.

'You remember when that incident occurred, Satterthwaite? *Just after Ellis had brought him a telephone message.* I think it's a fair deduction to assume that it was that telephone message which was the cause of Tollie's sudden unusual hilarity. You may remember I asked the housemaid woman what that message had been.'

Mr Satterthwaite nodded.

'It was to say that a woman named Mrs de Rushbridger had arrived at the Sanatorium,' he said, to show that he, too, had paid attention to the point. 'It doesn't sound particularly thrilling.'

'It doesn't sound so, certainly. But, if our reasoning is correct, *there must be some significance in that message.*'

'Ye-es,' said Mr Satterthwaite doubtfully.

'Indubitably,' said Sir Charles. 'We've got to find out what that significance was. It just crosses my mind that it may have been a code message of some kind – a harmless sounding natural thing, but which really meant something entirely different. If Tollie had been making inquiries into Babbington's death, this may have had something to do with those inquiries. Say, even, that he employed a private detective to find out a certain fact. He may have told him in the event of this particular suspicion being justified to ring up and use that particular phrase which would convey no hint of the truth to anyone taking it. That would explain his jubilation, it might explain his asking Ellis if he was sure of the name – he himself knowing well there was no such person, really. In fact, the slight lack of balance a person shows when they have brought off what can be described as a long shot.'

'You think there's no such person as Mrs de Rushbridger?'

'Well, I think we ought to find out for certain.'

'How?'

'We might run along to the Sanatorium now and ask the Matron.'

'She may think it rather odd.'

Sir Charles laughed.

'You leave it to me,' he said.

They turned aside from the drive and walked in the direction of the Sanatorium.

Mr Satterthwaite said:

'What about you, Cartwright? Does anything strike you at all? Arising out of our visit to the house, I mean.'

Sir Charles answered slowly.

'Yes, there is something – the devil of it is, I can't remember what.'

Mr Satterthwaite stared at him in surprise. The other frowned.

'How can I explain? There was something – something which at the moment struck me as wrong – as unlikely – only – I hadn't the time to think about it then. I put it aside in my own mind.'

'And now you can't remember what it was?'

'No – only that at some moment I said to myself, "That's odd."'

'Was it when we were questioning the servants? Which servant?'

'I tell you I can't remember. And the more I think the less I shall remember . . . If I leave it alone, it may come back to me.'

They came into view of the Sanatorium, a big white modern building, divided from the park by palings. There was a gate through which they passed, and they rang the front-door bell and asked for the Matron.

The Matron, when she came, was a tall, middle-aged woman, with an intelligent face and a capable manner. Sir Charles she clearly knew by name as a friend of the late Sir Bartholomew Strange.

Sir Charles explained that he had just come back from abroad, had been horrified to hear of his friend's death and of the terrible suspicions entertained, and had been up to the house to learn as many details as he could. The Matron spoke in moving terms of the loss Sir Bartholomew would be to them, and of his fine career as a doctor. Sir Charles professed himself anxious to know what was going to happen to the Sanatorium. The Matron explained that Sir Bartholomew had had two partners, both capable doctors, one was in residence at the Sanatorium.

'Bartholomew was very proud of this place, I know,' said Sir Charles.

'Yes, his treatments were a great success.'

'Mostly nerve cases, isn't it?'

'Yes.'

'That reminds me – fellow I met out at Monte had some kind of relation coming here. I forget her name now – odd sort of name – Rushbridger – Rusbrigger – something like that.'

'Mrs de Rushbridger, you mean?'

'That's it. Is she here now?'

'Oh, yes. But I'm afraid she won't be able to see you – not for some time yet. She's having a very strict rest cure.' The Matron smiled just a trifle archly. 'No letters, no exciting visitors . . .'

'I say, she's not very bad, is she?'

'Rather a bad nervous breakdown – lapses of memory, and severe nervous exhaustion. Oh, we shall get her right in time.'

The Matron smiled reassuringly.

'Let me see, haven't I heard Tollie – Sir Bartholomew – speak of her? She was a friend of his as well as a patient, wasn't she?'

'I don't think so, Sir Charles. At least the doctor never said so. She has recently arrived from the West Indies – really, it was very funny, I must tell you. Rather a difficult name for a servant to remember – the parlourmaid here is rather stupid. She came and said to me, "Mrs West India has come," and of course I suppose Rushbridger *does* sound rather like West India

– but it was rather a coincidence her having just come from the West Indies.'

'Rather – rather – most amusing. Her husband over, too?'

'He's still out there.'

'Ah, quite – quite. I must be mixing her up with someone else. It was a case the doctor was specially interested in?'

'Cases of amnesia are fairly common, but they're always interesting to a medical man – the variations, you know. Two cases are seldom alike.'

'Seems all very odd to me. Well, thank you, Matron, I'm glad to have had a little chat with you. I know how much Tollie thought of you. He often spoke about you,' finished Sir Charles mendaciously.

'Oh, I'm glad to hear that.' The Matron flushed and bridled. 'Such a splendid man – such a loss to us all. We were absolutely shocked – well, stunned would describe it better. Murder! Who ever would murder Dr Strange, I said. It's incredible. That awful butler. I hope the police catch him. And no motive or anything.'

Sir Charles shook his head sadly and they took their departure, going round by the road to the spot where the car awaited them.

In revenge for his enforced quiescence during the interview with the Matron, Mr Satterthwaite displayed a lively interest in the scene of Oliver Manders' accident, plying the lodge keeper, a slow-witted man of middle age, with questions.

Yes, that was the place, where the wall was broken away. On a motor cycle the young gentleman was. No, he didn't see it happen. He heard it, though, and come out to see. The young gentleman was standing there – just where the other gentleman was standing now. He didn't seem to be hurt. Just looking rueful-like at his bike – and a proper mess that was. Just asked what the name of the place might be, and when he heard it was Sir Bartholomew Strange's he said, 'That's a piece of luck,' and went on up to the house. A very calm young gentleman he seemed to be – tired like. How he come to have such an accident, the lodge keeper couldn't see, but he supposed them things went wrong sometimes.

'It was an odd accident,' said Mr Satterthwaite thoughtfully.

He looked at the wide straight road. No bends, no dangerous crossroads, nothing to cause a motor cyclist to swerve suddenly into a ten-foot wall. Yes, an odd accident.

'What's in your mind, Satterthwaite?' asked Sir Charles curiously.

'Nothing,' said Mr Satterthwaite, 'nothing.'

'It's odd, certainly,' said Sir Charles, and he, too, stared at the scene of the accident in a puzzled manner.

They got into the car and drove off.

Mr Satterthwaite was busy with his thoughts. Mrs de Rushbridger – Cartwright's theory wouldn't work – it wasn't a code message – there *was* such a person. But could there be something about the woman herself? Was she perhaps a witness of some kind, or was it just because she was an interesting case that Bartholomew Strange had displayed this unusual elation? Was she, perhaps, an attractive woman? To fall in love at the age of fifty-five did (Mr Satterthwaite had observed it many a time) change a man's character completely. It might, perhaps, make him facetious, where before he had been aloof –

His thoughts were interrupted. Sir Charles leant forward.

'Satterthwaite,' he said, 'do you mind if we turn back?'

'Without waiting for a reply, he took up the speaking tube and gave the order. The car slowed down, stopped, and the chauffeur began to reverse into a convenient lane. A minute or two later they were bowling along the road in the opposite direction.

'What is it?' asked Mr Satterthwaite.

'I've remembered,' said Sir Charles, 'what struck me as odd. It was the ink-stain on the floor in the butler's room.'

Chapter 6

Concerning An Ink-Stain

Mr Satterthwaite stared at his friend in surprise.

'The ink-stain?' What do you mean, Cartwright?'

'You remember it?'

'I remember there was an ink-stain, yes.'

'You remember its position?'

'Well – not exactly.'

'It was close to the skirting board near the fire-place.'

'Yes, so it was. I remember now.'

'How do you think that stain was caused, Satterthwaite?'

'It wasn't a big stain,' he said at last. 'It couldn't have been an upset ink-bottle. I should say in all probability that the man dropped his fountain pen there – there was no pen in the room, you remember.' (He shall see I notice things just as much as he does, thought Mr Satterthwaite.) 'So it seems clear the man must have had a fountain pen if he ever wrote at all – and there's no evidence that he ever did.'

'Yes, there is, Satterthwaite. There's the ink-stain.'

'He mayn't have been writing,' snapped Satterthwaite. 'He may have just droped the pen on the floor.'

'But there wouldn't have been a stain unless the top had been off the pen.'

'I daresay you're right,' said Mr Satterthwaite. 'But I can't see what's odd about it.'

'Perhaps there isn't anything odd,' said Sir Charles. 'I can't tell till I get back and see for myself.'

They were turning in at the lodge gates. A few minutes later they had arrived at the house and Sir Charles was allaying the curiosity caused by his return by inventing a pencil left behind in the butler's room.

'And now,' said Sir Charles, shutting the door of Ellis's room behind them, having with some skill shaken off the helpful Mrs Leckie, 'let's see if I'm making an infernal fool of myself, or whether there's anything in my idea.'

In Mr Satterthwaite's opinion the former alternative was by far the more probable, but he was much too polite to say so. He sat down on the bed and watched the other.

'Here's our stain,' said Sir Charles, indicating the mark with his foot. 'Right up against the skirting board at the opposite side of the room to the writing-table.

Under what circumstances would a man drop a pen just there?'

'You can drop a pen anywhere,' said Mr Satterthwaite.

'You can hurl it across the room, of course,' agreed Sir Charles. 'But one doesn't usually treat one's pen like that. I don't know, though. Fountain pens are damned annoying things. Dry up and refuse to write just when you want them to. Perhaps that's the solution of the matter. Ellis lost his temper, said, "Damn the thing," and hurled it across the room.'

'I think there are plenty of explanations,' said Mr Satterthwaite. 'He may have simply laid the pen on the mantelpiece and it rolled off.'

Sir Charles experimented with a pencil. He allowed it to roll off the corner of the mantelpiece. The pencil struck the ground at least a foot from the mark and rolled inwards towards the gas fire.

'Well,' said Mr Satterthwaite. 'What's your explanation?'

'I'm trying to find one.'

From his seat on the bed Mr Satterthwaite now witnessed a thoroughly amusing performance.

Sir Charles tried dropping the pencil from his hand as he walked in the direction of the fireplace. He tried sitting on the edge of the bed and writing there and then dropping the pencil. To get the pencil to fall on the right spot it was necessary to stand or sit jammed up against the wall in a most unconvincing attitude.

'That's impossible,' said Sir Charles aloud. He stood considering the wall, the stain and the prim little gas fire.

'If he were burning papers, now,' he said thoughtfully. 'But one doesn't burn papers in a gas fire –'

Suddenly he drew in his breath.

A minute later Mr Satterthwaite was realizing Sir Charles's profession to the full.

Charles Cartwright had become Ellis the butler. He sat writing at the writing-table. He looked furtive, every now and then he raised his eyes, shooting them shiftily from side to side. Suddenly he seemed to hear something – Mr Satterthwaite could even guess what that something was – footsteps along the passage. The man had a guilty conscience. He attached a certain meaning to those footsteps. He sprang up, the paper on which he had been writing in one hand, his pen in the other. He darted across the room to the fireplace, his head half turned, still alert – listening – afraid. He tried to shove the papers under the gas fire – in order to use both hands he cast down the pen impatiently. Sir Charles's pencil, the 'pen' of the drama, fell accurately on the ink-stain . . .

'Bravo,' said Mr Satterthwaite, applauding generously.

So good had the performance been that he was left with the impression that so and only so could Ellis have acted.

'You see?' said Sir Charles, resuming his own personality and speaking with modest elation. 'If the fellow heard the police or what he thought was the police coming and had to hide what he was writing – well, where could he hide it? Not in a drawer or under the mattress – if the police searched the room, that would be found at once. He hadn't time to take up a floor board. No, behind the gas fire was the only chance.'

'The next thing to do,' said Mr Satterthwaite, 'is to see whether there *is* anything hidden behind the gas fire.'

'Exactly. Of course, it may have been a false alarm, and he may have got the things out again later. But we'll hope for the best.'

'Removing his coat and turning up his shirt sleeves, Sir Charles lay down on the floor and applied his eye to the crack under the gas fire.

'There's something under there,' he reported. 'Something white. How can we get it out? We want something like a woman's hatpins.'

'Women don't have hatpins any more,' said Mr Satterthwaite sadly. 'Perhaps a penknife.'

But a penknife proved unavailing.

Agatha Christie

In the end Mr Satterthwaite went out and borrowed a knitting needle from Beatrice. Though extremely curious to know what he wanted it for, her sense of decorum was too great to permit her to ask.

The knitting needle did the trick. Sir Charles extracted half a dozen sheets of crumpled writing-paper, hastily crushed together and pushed in.

With growing excitement he and Mr Satterthwaite smoothed them out. They were clearly several different drafts of a letter – written in a small, neat clerkly handwriting.

This is to say (began the first) *that the writer of this does not wish to cause unpleasantness, and may possibly have been mistaken in what he thought he saw tonight, but –*

Here the writer had clearly been dissatisfied, and had broken off to start afresh.

John Ellis, butler, presents his compliments, and would be glad of a short interview touching the tragedy tonight before going to the police with certain information in his possession –

Still dissatisfied, the man had tried again.

John Ellis, butler, has certain facts concerning the death of the doctor in his possession. He has not yet given these facts to the police –

In the next one the use of the third person had been abandoned.

I am badly in need of money. A thousand pounds would make all the difference to me. There are certain things I could tell the police, but do not want to make trouble –

The last one was even more unreserved.

I know how the doctor died. I haven't said anything to the police – yet. If you will meet me –

This letter broke off in a different way – after the 'me' the pen had tailed off in a scrawl, and the last five words were all blurred and blotchy. Clearly it was when writing this that Ellis had heard something that alarmed him. He had crumpled up the papers and dashed to conceal them.

Mr Satterthwaite drew a deep breath.

'I congratulate you, Cartwright,' he said. 'Your instinct about that ink-stain was right. Good work. Now let's see exactly where we stand.'

He paused a minute.

'Ellis, as we thought, is a scoundrel. He wasn't the murderer, but he knew who the murderer was, and he was preparing to blackmail him or her –'

'Him or her,' interrupted Sir Charles. 'Annoying we don't know which. Why couldn't the fellow begin one of his effusions Sir or Madam, then we'd know where we are. Ellis seems to have been an artistic sort of fellow. He was taking a lot of trouble over his blackmailing letter. If only he'd given us one clue – as to whom that letter was addressed.'

'Never mind,' said Mr Satterthwaite. 'We are getting on. You remember you said that what we wanted to find in this room was a proof of Ellis's innocence. Well, we've found it. These letters show that he was innocent – of the murder, I mean. He was a thorough-paced scoundrel in other ways. But he didn't murder Sir Bartholomew Strange. Somebody else did that. Someone who murdered Babbington also. I think even the police will have to come round to our view now.'

'You're going to tell them about this?'

Sir Charles's voice expressed dissatisfaction.

'I don't see that we can do otherwise. Why?'

'Well –' Sir Charles sat down on the bed. His brow furrowed itself in thought. 'How can I put it best? At the moment we know something that nobody else does. The police are looking for Ellis. They think he's the murderer. Everyone knows that they think he's

Egg proved to be still in town. She and her mother were staying with relatives and were not returning to Loomouth for about a week. Egg was easily prevailed upon to come out and dine with the two men.

'She can't come here very well, I suppose,' said Sir Charles, looking round his luxurious flat. 'Her mother mightn't like it, eh? Of course we could have Miss Milray, too – but I'd rather not. To tell the truth, Miss Milray cramps my style a bit. She's so efficient that she gives me an inferiority complex.'

Mr Satterthwaite suggested his house. In the end it was arranged to dine at the Berkeley. Afterwards, if Egg liked, they could adjourn elsewhere.

Mr Satterthwaite noticed at once that the girl was looking thinner. Her eyes seemed larger and more feverish, her chin more decided. She was pale and had circles under her eyes. But her charm was as great as ever, her childish eagerness just as intense.

She said to Sir Charles, 'I knew you'd come . . .'

Her tone implied: 'Now that you've come everything will be all right . . .'

Mr Satterthwaite thought to himself: 'But she wasn't sure he'd come – she wasn't sure at all. She's been on tenterhooks. She's been fretting herself to death.' And he thought: 'Doesn't the man realize? Actors are usually vain enough . . . Doesn't he know the girl's head over ears in love with him?'

Agatha Christie

It was, he thought, an odd situation. That Sir Charles was overwhelmingly in love with the girl, he had no doubt whatever. She was equally in love with him. And the link between them – the link to which each of them clung frenziedly – was a crime – a double crime of a revolting nature.

During dinner little was said. Sir Charles talked about his experiences abroad. Egg talked about Loomouth. Mr Satterthwaite encouraged them both whenever the conversation seemed likely to flag. When dinner was over they went to Mr Satterthwaite's house.

Mr Satterthwaite's house was on Chelsea Embankment. It was a large house, and contained many beautiful works of art. There were pictures, sculpture, Chinese porcelain, prehistoric pottery, ivories, miniatures and much genuine Chippendale and Hepplewhite furniture. It had an atmosphere about it of mellowness and understanding.

Egg Lytton Gore saw nothing, noticed nothing. She flung off her evening coat on to a chair and said:

'At last. Now tell me all about it.'

She listened with vivid interest whilst Sir Charles narrated their adventures in Yorkshire, drawing in her breath sharply when he described the discovery of the blackmailing letters.

'What happened after that we can only conjecture,' finished Sir Charles. 'Presumably Ellis was paid to hold his tongue and his escape was facilitated.'

But Egg shook her head.

'Oh, no,' she said. 'Don't you see? *Ellis is dead.*'

Both men were startled, but Egg reiterated her assertion.

'Of course he's dead. That's why he's disappeared so successfully that no one can find a trace of him. He knew too much, and so he was killed. Ellis is the third murder.'

Although neither of the two men had considered the possibility before, they were forced to admit that it did not entirely ring false.

'But look here, my dear girl,' argued Sir Charles, 'it's all very well to say Ellis is dead. Where's the body? There's twelve stone or so of solid butler to be accounted for.'

'I don't know where the body is,' said Egg. 'There must be lots of places.'

'Hardly,' murmured Mr Satterthwaite. 'Hardly . . .'

'Lots,' reiterated Egg. 'Let me see . . .' She paused for a moment. 'Attics, there are masses of attics that no one ever goes into. He's probably in a trunk in the attic.'

'Rather unlikely,' said Sir Charles. 'But possible, of course. It might evade discovery – for – er – a time.'

It was not Egg's way to avoid unpleasantness. She dealt immediately with the point in Sir Charles's mind.

'Smell goes up, not down. You'd notice a decaying

body in the cellar much sooner than in the attic. And, anyway, for a long time people would think it was a dead rat.'

'If your theory were correct, it would point definitely to a man as the murderer. A woman couldn't drag a body round the house. In fact, it would be a pretty good feat for a man.'

'Well, there are other possibilities. There's a secret passage there, you know. Miss Sutcliffe told me so, and Sir Bartholomew told me he would show it to me. The murderer might have given Ellis the money and shown him the way to get out of the house – gone down the passage with him and killed him there. A woman could do that. She could stab him, or something, from behind. Then she'd just leave the body there and go back, and no one would ever know.'

Sir Charles shook his head doubtfully, but he no longer disputed Egg's theory.

Mr Satterthwaite felt sure that the same suspicion had come to him for a moment in Ellis's room when they had found the letters. He remembered Sir Charles's little shiver. The idea that Ellis might be dead had come to him then . . .

Mr Satterthwaite thought: 'If Ellis is dead, then we're dealing with a very dangerous person . . . Yes, a very dangerous person . . .' And suddenly he felt a cold chill of fear down his spine . . .

A person who had killed three times wouldn't hesitate to kill again . . .

They were in danger, all three of them – Sir Charles, and Egg, and he . . .

If they found out too much . . .

He was recalled by the sound of Sir Charles's voice.

'There's one thing I didn't understand in your letter, Egg. You spoke of Oliver Manders being in danger – of the police suspecting him. I can't see that they attach the least suspicion to him.'

It seemed to Mr Satterthwaite that Egg was very slightly discomposed. He even fancied that she blushed.

'Aha,' said Mr Satterthwaite to himself. 'Let's see how you get out of this, young lady.'

'It was silly of me,' said Egg. 'I got confused. I thought that Oliver arriving as he did, with what might have been a trumped-up excuse – well, I thought the police were sure to suspect him.'

Sir Charles accepted the explanation easily enough.

'Yes,' he said. 'I see.'

Mr Satterthwaite spoke.

'Was it a trumped-up excuse?' he said.

Egg turned on him.

'What do you mean?'

'It was an odd sort of accident,' said Mr Satterthwaite. 'I thought if it was a trumped-up excuse you might know.'

Egg shook her head.

Agatha Christie

'I don't know. I never thought about it. But why should Oliver pretend to have an accident if he didn't?'

'He might have had reasons,' said Sir Charles. 'Quite natural ones.'

He was smiling at her. Egg blushed crimson.

'Oh, no,' she said. '*No.*'

Sir Charles sighed. It occurred to Mr Satterthwaite that his friend had interpreted that blush quite wrongly. Sir Charles seemed a sadder and older man when he spoke again.

'Well,' he said, 'if our young friend is in no danger, where do I come in?'

Egg came forward quickly and caught him by the coat sleeve.

'You're not going away again. You're not going to give up? You're going to find out the truth – *the truth*. I don't believe anybody but you could find out the truth. You can. You will.'

She was tremendously in earnest. The waves of her vitality seemed to surge and eddy in the old-world air of the room.

'You believe in me?' said Sir Charles. He was moved.

'Yes, yes, yes. We're going to get at the truth. You and I together.'

'And Satterthwaite.'

'Of course, and Mr Satterthwaite,' said Egg without interest.

148

Mr Satterthwaite smiled covertly. Whether Egg wanted to include him or not, he had no intention of being left out. He was fond of mysteries, and he liked observing human nature, and he had a soft spot for lovers. All three tastes seemed likely to be gratified in this affair.

Sir Charles sat down. His voice changed. He was in command, directing a production.

'First of all we've got to clarify the situation. Do we, or do we not, believe that the same person killed Babbington and Bartholomew Strange?'

'Yes,' said Egg.

'Yes,' said Mr Satterthwaite.

'Do we believe that the second murder sprang directly from the first? I mean, do we believe that Bartholomew Strange was killed in order to prevent his revealing the facts of the first murder, or his suspicion about it?'

'Yes,' said Egg and Mr Satterthwaite again, but in unison this time.

'Then it is the *first* murder we must investigate, not the second –'

Egg nodded.

'In my mind, until we discover the *motive* for the first murder, we can hardly hope to discover the murderer. The motive presents extraordinary difficulty. Babbington was a harmless, pleasant, gentle old man without, one would say, an enemy in the world. Yet he was killed – and there must have been some *reason* for the killing. We've got to find that reason.'

He paused and then said in his ordinary everyday voice:

'Let's get down to it. What reasons are there for killing people? First, I suppose, gain.'

'Revenge,' said Egg.

'Homicidal mania,' said Mr Satterthwaite. 'The *crime passionel* would hardly apply in this case. But there's fear.'

Charles Cartwright nodded. He was scribbling on a piece of paper.

'That about covers the ground,' he said. 'First, *Gain*. Does anyone gain by Babbington's death? Has he any money – or expectation of money?'

'I should think it very unlikely,' said Egg.

'So should I, but we'd better approach Mrs Babbington on the point.'

'Then there's revenge. Did Babbington do any injury to anyone – perhaps in his young days? Did he marry the girl that some other man wanted? We'll have to look into that, too.'

'Then homicidal mania. Were both Babbington and Tollie killed by a lunatic? I don't think that theory will hold water. Even a lunatic has some kind of reasonableness in his crimes. I mean a lunatic might think himself divinely appointed to kill doctors, or to kill clergymen, but not to kill both. I think we can wash out the theory of homicidal mania. There remains *fear*.

'Now, frankly, that seems to me far the most likely solution. Babbington knew something about somebody – or he recognized somebody. He was killed to prevent him telling what that something was.'

'I can't see what someone like Mr Babbington could know that was damaging about anybody who was there that night.'

'Perhaps,' said Sir Charles, 'it was something that he didn't know that he knew.'

He went on, trying to make his meaning clear.

'It's difficult to say just what I mean. Suppose, for instance (this is only an instance) that Babbington saw a certain person in a certain place at a certain time. As far as he knows, there's no reason why that person shouldn't be there. But suppose also that that person had concocted a very clever alibi for some reason showing that at that particular time he was somewhere else a hundred miles away. Well, at any minute old Babbington, in the most innocent way in the world, might give the show away.'

'*I* see,' said Egg. 'Say there's a murder committed in London, and Babbington sees the man who did it at Paddington Station, but the man has proved that he didn't do it by having an alibi showing that he was at Leeds at the time. Then Babbington might give the whole show away.'

151

'That's what I mean exactly. Of course that's only an instance. It might be anything. Someone he saw that evening whom he'd known under a different name –'

'It might be something to do with a marriage,' said Egg. 'Clergymen do lots of marriages. Somebody who'd committed bigamy.'

'Or it might have to do with a birth or a death,' suggested Mr Satterthwaite.

'It's a very wide field,' said Egg, frowning. 'We'll have to get at it the other way. Work back from the people who were there. Let's make a list. Who was at your house, and who was at Sir Bartholomew's.'

She took the paper and pencil from Sir Charles.

'The Dacres, they were at both. That woman like a wilted cabbage, what's her name – Wills. Miss Sutcliffe.'

'You can leave Angela out of it,' said Sir Charles. 'I've known her for years.'

Egg frowned mutinously.

'We can't do that sort of thing,' she said. 'Leave people out because we know them. We've got to be business-like. Besides, *I* don't know anything about Angela Sutcliffe. She's just as likely to have done it as anyone else, so far as I can see – more likely. All actresses have pasts. I think, on the whole, she's the most likely person.'

She gazed defiantly at Sir Charles. There was an answering spark in his eyes.

'In that case we mustn't leave out Oliver Manders.'

'How could it be Oliver? He'd met Mr Babbington ever so many times before.'

'He was at both places, and his arrival is a little – open to suspicion.'

'Very well,' said Egg. She paused, and then added: 'In that case I'd better put down Mother and myself as well . . . That makes six suspects.'

'I don't think –'

'We'll do it properly, or not at all.' Her eyes flashed.

Mr Satterthwaite made peace by offering refreshment. He rang for drinks.

Sir Charles strolled off into a far corner to admire a head of Negro sculpture. Egg came over to Mr Satterthwaite and slipped a hand through his arm.

'Stupid of me to have lost my temper,' she murmured. 'I *am* stupid – but why should the woman be excepted? Why is he so keen she should be? Oh, dear, why the devil am I so disgustingly jealous?'

Mr Satterthwaite smiled and patted her hand.

'Jealousy never pays, my dear,' he said. 'If you feel jealous, don't show it. By the way, did you really think young Manders might be suspected?'

Egg grinned – a friendly childish grin.

'Of course not. I put that in so as not to alarm the

man.' She turned her head. Sir Charles was still moodily studying Negro sculpture. 'You know – I didn't want him to think I really have a pash for Oliver – because I haven't. How difficult everything is! He's gone back now to his "Bless you, my children," attitude. I don't want that at all.'

'Have patience,' counselled Mr Satterthwaite. 'Everything comes right in the end, you know.'

'I'm not patient,' said Egg. 'I want to have things at once, or even quicker.'

Mr Satterthwaite laughed, and Sir Charles turned and came towards them.

As they sipped their drinks, they arranged a plan of campaign. Sir Charles should return to Crow's Nest, for which he had not yet found a purchaser. Egg and her mother would return to Rose Cottage rather sooner than they had meant to do. Mrs Babbington was still living in Loomouth. They would get what information they could from her and then proceed to act upon it.

'We'll succeed,' said Egg. 'I know we'll succeed.'

She leaned forward to Sir Charles, her eyes glowing. She held out her glass to touch his.

'Drink to our success,' she commanded.

Slowly, very slowly, his eyes fixed on hers, he raised his glass to his lips.

'To success,' he said, 'and to the Future . . .'

Third Act

Discovery

Third Act

Discovery

Chapter 1

Mrs Babbington

Mrs Babbington had moved into a small fisherman's cottage not far from the harbour. She was expecting a sister home from Japan in about six months. Until her sister arrived she was making no plans for the future. The cottage chanced to be vacant, and she took it for six months. She felt too bewildered by her sudden loss to move away from Loomouth. Stephen Babbington had held the living of St Petroch, Loomouth, for seventeen years. They had been, on the whole, seventeen happy and peaceful years, in spite of the sorrow occasioned by the death of her son Robin. Of her remaining children, Edward was in Ceylon, Lloyd was in South Africa, and Stephen was third officer on the *Angolia*. They wrote frequently and affectionately, but they could offer neither a home nor companionship to their mother.

Margaret Babbington was very lonely . . . .

Not that she allowed herself much time for thinking. She was still active in the parish – the new vicar was unmarried, and she spent a good deal of time working in the tiny plot of ground in front of the cottage. She was a woman whose flowers were part of her life.

She was working there one afternoon when she heard the latch of the gate click, and looked up to see Sir Charles Cartwright and Egg Lytton Gore.

Margaret was not surprised to see Egg. She knew that the girl and her mother were due to return shortly. But she was surprised to see Sir Charles. Rumour had insisted that he had left the neighbourhood for good. There had been paragraphs copied from other papers about his doings in the South of France. There had been a board 'TO BE SOLD' stuck up in the garden of Crow's Nest. No one had expected Sir Charles to return. Yet return he had.

Mrs Babbington shook the untidy hair back from her hot forehead and looked ruefully at her earth-stained hands.

'I'm not fit to shake hands,' she said. 'I ought to garden in gloves, I know. I do start in them sometimes; but I always tear them off sooner or later. One can feel things so much better with bare hands.'

She led the way into the house. The tiny sitting-room had been made cosy with chintz. There were photographs and bowls of chrysanthemums.

'It's a great surprise seeing you, Sir Charles. I thought you had given up Crow's Nest for good.'

'I thought I had,' said the actor frankly. 'But sometimes, Mrs Babbington, our destiny is too strong for us.'

Mrs Babbington did not reply. She turned towards Egg, but the girl forestalled the words on her lips.

'Look here, Mrs Babbington. This isn't just a call. Sir Charles and I have got something very serious to say. Only – I – I should hate to upset you.'

Mrs Babbington looked from the girl to Sir Charles. Her face had gone rather grey and pinched.

'First of all,' said Sir Charles, 'I would like to ask you if you have had any communication from the Home Office?'

Mrs Babbington bowed her head.

'I see – well, perhaps that makes what we are about to say easier.'

'Is that what you have come about – this exhumation order?'

'Yes. Is it – I'm afraid it must be – very distressing to you.'

She softened to the sympathy in his voice.

'Perhaps I do not mind as much as you think. To some people the idea of exhumation is very dreadful – not to me. It is not the dead clay that matters. My dear husband is elsewhere – at peace – where no one can trouble his rest. No, it is not that. It is the idea that is a shock to me – the idea, a terrible one, that Stephen did not die a natural death. It seems so impossible – utterly impossible.'

'I'm afraid it must seem so to you. It did to me – to us – at first.'

'What do you mean by at first, Sir Charles?'

'Because the suspicion crossed my mind on the evening of your husband's death, Mrs Babbington. Like you, however, it seemed to me so impossible that I put it aside.'

'I thought so, too,' said Egg.

'You too,' Mrs Babbington looked at her wonderingly. 'You thought someone could have killed – Stephen?'

The incredulity in her voice was so great that neither of her visitors knew quite how to proceed. At last Sir Charles took up the tale.

'As you know, Mrs Babbington, I went abroad. When I was in the South of France I read in the paper of my friend Bartholomew Strange's death in almost exactly similar circumstances. I also got a letter from Miss Lytton Gore.'

Egg nodded.

'I was there, you know, staying with him at the time. Mrs Babbington, it was exactly the same – *exactly*. He drank some port and his face changed, and – and

– well, it was just the same. He died two or three minutes later.'

Mrs Babbington shook her head slowly.

'I can't understand it. Stephen! Sir Bartholomew – a kind and clever doctor! Who could want to harm either of them? It must be a mistake.'

'Sir Bartholomew was proved to have been poisoned, remember,' said Sir Charles.

'Then it must have been the work of a lunatic.'

Sir Charles went on:

'Mrs Babbington, I want to get to the bottom of this. I want to find out the truth. And I feel there is no time to lose. Once the news of the exhumation gets about our criminal will be on the alert. I am assuming, for the sake of saving time, what the result of the autopsy on your husband's body will be. I am taking it that he, too, died of nicotine poisoning. To begin with, did you or he know anything about the use of pure nicotine?'

'I always use a solution of nicotine for spraying roses. I didn't know it was supposed to be poisonous.'

'I should imagine (I was reading up the subject last night) that in both cases the pure alkaloid must have been used. Cases of poisoning by nicotine are most unusual.'

Mrs Babbington shook her head.

Agatha Christie

'I really don't know anything about nicotine poisoning – except that I suppose inveterate smokers might suffer from it.'

'Did your husband smoke?'

'Yes.'

'Now tell me, Mrs Babbington, you have expressed the utmost surprise that anyone should want to do away with your husband. Does that mean that as far as you know he had no enemies?'

'I am sure Stephen had no enemies. Everyone was fond of him. People tried to hustle him sometimes,' she smiled a little tearfully. 'He was getting on, you know, and rather afraid of innovations, but everybody liked him. You couldn't dislike Stephen, Sir Charles.'

'I suppose, Mrs Babbington, that your husband didn't leave very much money?'

'No. Next to nothing. Stephen was not good at saving. He gave away far too much. I used to scold him about it.'

'I suppose he had no expectations from anyone? He wasn't the heir to any property?'

'Oh, no. Stephen hadn't many relations. He has a sister who is married to a clergyman in Northumberland, but they are very badly off, and all his uncles and aunts are dead.'

'Then it does not seem as though there were anyone who could benefit by Mr Babbington's death?'

'No, indeed.'

'Let us come back to the question of enemies for a minute. Your husband had no enemies, you say; but he may have had as a young man.'

Mrs Babbington looked sceptical.

'I should think it very unlikely. Stephen hadn't a quarrelsome nature. He always got on well with people.'

'I don't want to sound melodramatic,' Sir Charles coughed a little nervously. 'But – er – when he got engaged to you, for instance, there wasn't any disappointed suitor in the offing?'

A momentary twinkle came into Mrs Babbington's eyes.

'Stephen was my father's curate. He was the first young man I saw when I came home from school. I fell in love with him and he with me. We were engaged for four years, and then he got a living down in Kent, and we were able to get married. Ours was a very simple love story, Sir Charles – and a very happy one.'

Sir Charles bowed his head. Mrs Babbington's simple dignity was very charming.

Egg took up the rôle of questioner.

'Mrs Babbington, do you think your husband had met any of the guests at Sir Charles's that night before?'

Mrs Babbington looked slightly puzzled.

'Well, there were you and your mother, my dear, and young Oliver Manders.'

'Yes, but any of the others?'

'We had both seen Angela Sutcliffe in a play in London five years ago. Both Stephen and I were very excited that we were actually going to meet her.'

'You had never actually met her before?'

'No. We've never met any actresses – or actors, for the matter of that – until Sir Charles came to live here. And that,' added Mrs Babbington, 'was a great excitement. I don't think Sir Charles knows what a wonderful thing it was to us. Quite a breath of romance in our lives.'

'You hadn't met Captain and Mrs Dacres?'

'Was he the little man, and the woman with the wonderful clothes?'

'Yes.'

'No. Nor the other woman – the one who wrote plays. Poor thing, she looked rather out of it, I thought.'

'You're sure you'd never seen any of them before?'

'I'm quite sure I hadn't – and so I'm fairly sure Stephen hadn't, either. You see, we do everything together.'

'And Mr Babbington didn't say anything to you – anything at all,' persisted Egg, 'about the people you were going to meet, or about them, when he saw them?'

'Nothing beforehand – except that he was looking forward to an interesting evening. And when we got there – well, there wasn't much time –' Her face twisted suddenly.

Sir Charles broke in quickly.

'You must forgive us badgering you like this. But, you see, we feel that there must be *something*, if only we could get at it. There must be some *reason* for an apparently brutal and meaningless murder.'

'I see that,' said Mrs Babbington. 'If it was murder, there must be some reason . . . But I don't know – I can't imagine – what that reason could be.'

There was silence for a minute or two, then Sir Charles said:

'Can you give me a slight biographical sketch of your husband's career?'

Mrs Babbington had a good memory for dates. Sir Charles's final notes ran thus:

'Stephen Babbington, born Islington, Devon, 1868. Educated St Paul's School and Oxford. Ordained Deacon and received a title to the Parish of Hoxton, 1891. Priested 1892. Was Curate Eslington, Surrey, to Rev. Vernon Lorrimer, 1894–1899. Married Margaret Lorrimer, 1899, and presented to the living of Gilling, Kent. Transferred to living of St Petroch, Loomouth, 1916.'

'That gives us something to go upon,' said Sir

Charles. 'Our best chance seems to me the time during which Mr Babbington was Vicar of St Mary's, Gilling. His earlier history seems rather far back to concern any of the people who were at my house that evening.'

Mrs Babbington shuddered.

'Do you really think – that one of them –?'

'I don't know what to think,' said Sir Charles. 'Bartholomew saw something or guessed something, and Bartholomew Strange died the same way, and five –'

'Seven,' said Egg.

'– of these people were also present. One of them must be guilty.'

'But why?' cried Mrs Babbington. 'Why? What motive could there be for anyone killing Stephen?'

'That,' said Sir Charles, 'is what we are going to find out.'

Chapter 2
Lady Mary

Mr Satterthwaite had come down to Crow's Nest with Sir Charles. Whilst his host and Egg Lytton Gore were visiting Mrs Babbington, Mr Satterthwaite was having tea with Lady Mary.

Lady Mary liked Mr Satterthwaite. For all her gentleness of manner, she was a woman who had very definite views on the subject of whom she did or did not like.

Mr Satterthwaite sipped China tea from a Dresden cup, and ate a microscopic sandwich and chatted. On his last visit they had found many friends and acquaintances in common. Their talk today began on the same subject, but gradually drifted into more intimate channels. Mr Satterthwaite was a sympathetic person – he listened to the troubles of other people and did not intrude his own. Even on his last visit it had seemed natural to Lady Mary to speak to him of her preoccupation with her daughter's future. She talked now as she would have talked to a friend of many years' standing.

'Egg is so headstrong,' she said. 'She flings herself into a thing heart and soul. You know, Mr Satterthwaite, I do not like the way she is – well, mixing herself up in this distressing business. It – Egg would laugh at me, I know – but it doesn't seem to be ladylike.'

She flushed as she spoke. Her brown eyes, gentle and ingenuous, looked with childish appeal at Mr Satterthwaite.

'I know what you mean,' he said. 'I confess that I don't quite like it myself. I know that it's simply an old-fashioned prejudice, but there it is. All the same,' he twinkled at her, 'we can't expect young ladies to sit at home and sew and shudder at the idea of crimes of violence in these enlightened days.'

'I don't like to think of murder,' said Lady Mary. 'I never, never dreamed that I should be mixed up in anything of that kind. It was dreadful.' She shivered. 'Poor Sir Bartholomew.'

'You didn't know him very well?' hazarded Mr Satterthwaite.

'I think I'd only met him twice. The first time about a year ago, when he came down to stay with Sir Charles for a weekend, and the second time was on that dreadful evening when poor Mr Babbington died. I was really most surprised when his invitation arrived. I accepted because I thought Egg would enjoy it. She hasn't many treats, poor child, and – well, she had seemed a little down in the mouth, as though she didn't take any interest in anything. I thought a big house-party might cheer her up.'

Mr Satterthwaite nodded.

'Tell me something about Oliver Manders,' he said. 'The young fellow rather interests me.'

'I think he's clever,' said Lady Mary. 'Of course, things have been difficult for him . . .'

She flushed, and then in answer to the plain inquiry of Mr Satterthwaite's glance she went on.

'You see, his father wasn't married to his mother . . .'

'Really? I had no idea of that.'

'Everyone knows about it down here, otherwise I wouldn't have said anything about it. Old Mrs Manders, Oliver's grandmother, lives at Dunboyne, that biggish house on the Plymouth road. Her husband was a lawyer down here. Her son went into a city firm and did very well. He's quite a rich man. The daughter was a good-looking girl, and she became absolutely infatuated with a married man. I blame him very much indeed. Anyway, in the end, after a lot of scandal, they went off together. His wife wouldn't divorce him. The girl died not long after Oliver was born. His uncle in London took charge of him. He and his wife had no

Agatha Christie

children of their own. The boy divided his time between them and his grandmother. He always came down here for his summer holidays.'

She paused and then went on:

'I always felt sorry for him. I still do. I think that terribly conceited manner of his is a good deal put on.'

'I shouldn't be surprised,' said Mr Satterthwaite. 'It's a very common phenomenon. If I ever see anyone who appears to think a lot of themselves and boasts unceasingly, I always know that there's a secret sense of inferiority somewhere.'

'It seems very odd.'

'An inferiority complex is a very peculiar thing. Crippen, for instance, undoubtedly suffered from it. It's at the back of a lot of crimes. The desire to assert one's personality.'

'It seems very strange to me,' murmured Lady Mary.

She seemed to shrink a little. Mr Satterthwaite looked at her with an almost sentimental eye. He liked her graceful figure with the sloping shoulders, the soft brown of her eyes, her complete absence of make-up. He thought:

'She must have been a beauty when she was young . . .'

Not a flaunting beauty, not a rose – no, a modest, charming violet, hiding its sweetness . . .

His thoughts ran serenely in the idiom of his young days . . .

He remembered incidents in his own youth.

Presently he found himself telling Lady Mary about his own love affair – the only love affair he had ever had. Rather a poor love affair by the standards of today, but very dear to Mr Satterthwaite.

He told her about the Girl, and how pretty she was, and of how they had gone together to see the bluebells at Kew. He had meant to propose to her that day. He had imagined (so he put it) that she reciprocated his sentiments. And then, as they were standing looking at the bluebells, she had confided in him . . . He had discovered that she loved another. And he had hidden the thoughts surging in his breast and had taken up the rôle of the faithful Friend.

It was not, perhaps, a very full-blooded romance, but it sounded well in the dim-faded chintz and egg-shell china atmosphere of Lady Mary's drawing-room.

Afterwards Lady Mary spoke of her own life, of her married life, which had not been very happy.

'I was such a foolish girl – girls are foolish, Mr Satterthwaite. They are so sure of themselves, so convinced they know best. People write and talk a lot of a "woman's instinct". I don't believe, Mr Satterthwaite, that there is any such thing. There doesn't seem to be anything that warns girls against a certain type of man. Nothing in themselves, I mean. Their parents warn them, but that's no good – one doesn't believe. It seems dreadful to say so, but there is something attractive to a girl in being told anyone is a bad man. She thinks at once that her love will reform him.'

Mr Satterthwaite nodded gently.

'One knows so little. When one knows more, it is too late.'

She sighed.

'It was all my own fault. My people didn't want me to marry Ronald. He was well born, but he had a bad reputation. My father told me straight out that he was a wrong 'un. I didn't believe it. I believed that, for my sake, he would turn over a new leaf . . .'

She was silent a moment or two, dwelling on the past.

'Ronald was a very fascinating man. My father was quite right about him. I soon found that out. It's an old-fashioned thing to say – but he broke my heart. Yes, he broke my heart. I was always afraid – of what might come out next.'

Mr Satterthwaite, always intensely interested in other people's lives, made a cautious sympathetic noise.

'It may seem a very wicked thing to say, Mr Satterthwaite, but it was a relief when he got pneumonia and died . . . Not that I didn't care for him – I loved him up to the end – but I had no illusions about him any longer. And there was Egg –'

Her voice softened.

Such a funny little thing she was. A regular little roly-poly, trying to stand up and falling over – just like an egg; that's how that ridiculous nickname started . . .'

She paused again.

'Some books that I've read these last few years have brought a lot of comfort to me. Books on psychology. It seems to show that in many ways people can't help themselves. A kind of kink. Sometimes, in the most carefully brought-up families you get it. As a boy Ronald stole money at school – money that he didn't need. I can feel now that he couldn't help himself . . . He was born with a kink . . .'

Very gently, with a small handkerchief, Lady Mary wiped her eyes.

'It wasn't what I was brought up to believe,' she said apologetically. 'I was taught that everyone knew the difference between right and wrong. But somehow – I don't always think that is so.'

'The human mind is a great mystery,' said Mr Satterthwaite gently. 'As yet, we are going groping our way to understanding. Without acute mania it may nevertheless occur that certain natures lack what I should describe as braking power. If you or I were to say, "I hate someone – I wish he were dead," the idea would pass from our minds as soon as the words were uttered. The brakes would work automatically. But, in some people the idea, or obsession, holds.

They see nothing but the immediate gratification of the idea formed.'

'I'm afraid,' said Lady Mary, 'that that's rather too clever for me.'

'I apologize. I was talking rather bookishly.'

'Did you mean that young people have too little restraint nowadays? It sometimes worries me.'

'No, no, I didn't mean that at all. Less restraint is, I think, a good thing – wholesome. I suppose you are thinking of Miss – er – Egg.'

'I think you'd better call her Egg,' said Lady Mary, smiling.

'Thank you. Miss Egg does sound rather ridiculous.'

'Egg's very impulsive, and once she has set her mind on a thing nothing will stop her. As I said before, I hate her mixing herself up in all this, but she won't listen to me.'

Mr Satterthwaite smiled at the distress in Lady Mary's tone. He thought to himself:

'I wonder if she realizes for one minute that Egg's absorption in crime is neither more nor less than a new variant of that old, old game – the pursuit of the male by the female? No, she'd be horrified at the thought.'

'Egg says that Mr Babbington was poisoned also. Do you think that is true, Mr Satterthwaite? Or do you think it is just one of Egg's sweeping statements?'

'We shall know for certain after the exhumation.'

'There is to be an exhumation, then?' Lady Mary shivered. 'How terrible for poor Mrs Babbington. I can imagine nothing more awful for any woman.'

'You knew the Babbingtons fairly intimately, I suppose, Lady Mary?'

'Yes, indeed. They are – were – very dear friends of ours.'

'Do you know of anyone who could possibly have had a grudge against the vicar?'

'No, indeed.'

'He never spoke of such a person?'

'No.'

'And they got on well together?'

'They were perfectly mated – happy in each other and in their children. They were badly off, of course, and Mr Babbington suffered from rheumatoid arthritis. Those were their only troubles.'

'How did Oliver Manders get on with the vicar?'

'Well –' Lady Mary hesitated, 'they didn't hit it off very well. The Babbingtons were sorry for Oliver, and he used to go to the vicarage a good deal in the holidays to play with the Babbington boys – though I don't think he got on very well with them. Oliver wasn't exactly a popular boy. He boasted too much of the money he had and the tuck he took back to school, and all the fun he had in London. Boys are rather merciless about that sort of thing.'

'Yes, but later – since he's been grown up?'

'I don't think he and the vicarage people have seen much of each other. As a matter of fact Oliver was rather rude to Mr Babbington one day here, in my house. It was about two years ago.'

'What happened?'

'Oliver made a rather ill-bred attack on Christianity. Mr Babbington was very patient and courteous with him. That only seemed to make Oliver worse. He said, "All you religious people look down your noses because my father and mother weren't married. I suppose you'd call me the child of sin. Well, I admire people who have the courage of their convictions and don't care what a lot of hypocrites and parsons think." Mr Babbington didn't answer, but Oliver went on: "You won't answer that. It's ecclesiasticism and supersitition that's got the whole world into the mess it's in. I'd like to sweep away the churches all over the world." Mr Babbington smiled and said, "And the clergy, too?" I think it was his smile that annoyed Oliver. He felt he was not being taken seriously. He said, "I hate everything the Church stands for. Smugness, security and hypocrisy. Get rid of the whole canting tribe, I say!" And Mr Babbington smiled – he had a very sweet smile – and he said, "My dear boy, if you were to sweep away all the churches ever built or planned, you would still have to reckon with God."'

'What did young Manders say to that?'

'He seemed taken aback, and then he recovered his temper and went back to his usual sneering tired manner.

'He said, "I'm afraid the things I've been saying are rather bad form, padre, and not very easily assimilated by your generation."'

'You don't like young Manders, do you, Lady Mary?'

'I'm sorry for him,' said Lady Mary defensively.

'But you wouldn't like him to marry Egg.'

'Oh, no.'

'I wonder why, exactly?'

'Because – because, he isn't *kind* . . . and because –'

'Yes?'

'Because there's something in him, somewhere, that I don't understand. Something *cold* –'

Mr Satterthwaite looked at her thoughtfully for a minute or two, then he said:

'What did Sir Bartholomew Strange think of him? Did he ever mention him?'

'He said, I remember, that he found young Manders an interesting study. He said that he reminded him of a case he was treating at the moment in his nursing home. I said that I thought Oliver looked particularly strong and healthy, and he said, "Yes, his health's all right, but he's riding for a fall."'

Agatha Christie

She paused and then said:

'I suppose Sir Bartholomew was a very clever nerve specialist.'

'I believe he was very highly thought of by his own colleagues.'

'I liked him,' said Lady Mary.

'Did he ever say anything to you about Babbington's death?'

'No.'

'He never mentioned it at all?'

'I don't think so.'

'Do you think – it's difficult for you to tell, not knowing him well – but do you think he had anything on his mind?'

'He seemed in very good spirits – even amused by something – some private joke of his own. He told me at dinner that night that he was going to spring a surprise on me.'

'Oh, he did, did he?'

On his way home, Mr Satterthwaite pondered that statement.

What had been the surprise Sir Bartholomew had intended to spring on his guests?

Would it, when it came, have been as amusing as he pretended?

Or did that gay manner mask a quiet but indomitable purpose? Would anyone ever know?

Chapter 3

Re-Enter Hercule Poirot

'Frankly,' said Sir Charles, 'are we any forrader?'

It was a council of war. Sir Charles, Mr Satterthwaite and Egg Lytton Gore were sitting in the Ship-room. A fire burned in the grate, and outside an equinoctial gale was howling.

Mr Satterthwaite and Egg answered the question simultaneously.

'No,' said Mr Satterthwaite.

'Yes,' said Egg.

Sir Charles looked from one to the other of them. Mr Satterthwaite indicated gracefully that the lady should speak first.

Egg was silent a moment or two, collecting her ideas.

'We *are* further on,' she said at last. 'We are further on because we haven't found out anything. That sounds nonsense, but it isn't. What I mean is that we had certain vague sketchy ideas; we know now that certain of those ideas are definitely washouts.'

'Progress by elimination,' said Sir Charles.

'That's it.'

Mr Satterthwaite cleared his throat. He liked to define things.

'The idea of gain we can now put definitely away,' he said. 'There does not seem to be anybody who (in detective story parlance) could benefit by Stephen Babbington's death. Revenge seems equally out of the question. Apart from his naturally amiable and peace-loving disposition, I doubt if he were *important* enough to make enemies. So we are back at our last rather sketchy idea – fear. By the death of Stephen Babbington, someone gains security.'

'That's rather well put,' said Egg.

Mr Satterthwaite looked modestly pleased with himself. Sir Charles looked a little annoyed. His was the star part, not Satterthwaite's.

'The point is,' said Egg, 'what are we going to do next – actually *do*, I mean. Are we going to sleuth people, or what? Are we going to disguise ourselves and follow them?'

'My dear child,' said Sir Charles, 'I always did set my face against playing old men in beards, and I'm not going to begin now.'

'Then what –?' began Egg.

But she was interrupted. The door opened, and Temple announced:

'Mr Hercule Poirot.'

M. Poirot walked in with a beaming face and greeted three highly astonished people.

'It is permitted,' he said with a twinkle, 'that I assist at this conference? I am right, am I not – it is a conference?'

'My dear fellow, we're delighted to see you.' Sir Charles, recovering from his surprise, shook his guest warmly by the hand and pushed him into a large arm-chair. 'Where have you sprung from so suddenly?'

'I went to call upon my good friend Mr Satterthwaite in London. They tell me he is away – in Cornwall. *Eh bien*, it leaps to the eye where he has gone. I take the first train to Loomouth, and here I am.'

'Yes,' said Egg. 'But why have you come?'

'I mean,' she went on, flushing a little as she realized the possible discourtesy of her words, 'you have come for some particular reason?'

'I have come,' said Hercule Poirot, 'to admit an error.'

With an engaging smile he turned to Sir Charles and spread out his hands in a foreign gesture.

'Monsieur, it was in this very room that you declared yourself not satisfied. And I – I thought it was your dramatic instinct – I said to myself, he is a great actor, at all costs he must have drama. It seemed, I will admit it, incredible that a harmless old gentleman should have died anything but a natural death. Even now I do not see how poison could have been administered to him, nor can I guess at any motive. It seems absurd – fantastic. And yet – since then, there has been another death, a death under similar circumstances. One cannot attribute it to coincidence. No, there must be a link between the two. And so, Sir Charles, I have come to you to apologize – to say I, Hercule Poirot, was wrong, and to ask you to admit me to your councils.'

Sir Charles cleared his throat rather nervously. He looked a little embarrassed.

'That's extraordinarily handsome of you, M. Poirot. I don't know – taking up a lot of your time – I –'

He stopped, somewhat at a loss. His eyes consulted Mr Satterthwaite.

'It is very good of you—' began Mr Satterthwaite.

'No, no, it is not good of me. It is the curiosity – and, yes, the hurt to my pride. I must repair my fault. My time – that is nothing – why voyage after all? The language may be different, but everywhere human nature is the same. But of course if I am not welcome, if you feel that I intrude –'

Both men spoke at once.

'No, indeed.'

'Rather not.'

Poirot turned his eyes to the girl.

'And Mademoiselle?'

For a minute or two Egg was silent, and on all three men the same impression was produced. *Egg did not want the assistance of M. Poirot . . .*

Mr Satterthwaite thought he knew why. This was the private ploy of Charles Cartwright and Egg Lytton Gore. Mr Satterthwaite had been admitted – on sufferance – on the clear understanding that he was a negligible third party. But Hercule Poirot was different. His would be the leading rôle. Perhaps, even, Sir Charles might retire in his favour. And then Egg's plans would come to naught.

He watched the girl, sympathizing with her predicament. These men did not understand, but he, with his semi-feminine sensitiveness, realized her dilemma. Egg was fighting for her happiness . . .

What would she say?

After all what could she say? How could she speak the thoughts in her mind? *'Go away – go away – your coming may spoil everything – I don't want you here . . .'*

Egg Lytton Gore said the only thing she could say.

'Of course,' she said with a little smile. 'We'd love to have you.'

Chapter 4

A Watching Brief

'Good,' said Poirot. 'We are colleagues. *Eh bien*, you will put me, if you please, *au courant* of the situation.'

He listened with close attention whilst Mr Satterthwaite outlined the steps they had taken since returning to England. Mr Satterthwaite was a good narrator. He had the faculty of creating an atmosphere, of painting a picture. His description of the Abbey, of the servants, of the Chief Constable was admirable. Poirot was warm in his appreciation of the discovery by Sir Charles of the unfinished letters under the gas fire.

'*Ah, mais c'est magnifique, ça!*' he exclaimed ecstatically. 'The deduction, the reconstruction – perfect! You should have been a great detective, Sir Charles, instead of a great actor.'

Sir Charles received these plaudits with becoming modesty – his own particular brand of modesty. He had not received compliments on his stage performances for many years without perfecting a manner of acknowledging them.

'Your observation, too, it was very just,' said Poirot, turning to Mr Satterthwaite. 'That point of yours about his sudden familiarity with the butler.'

'Do you think there is anything in this Mrs de Rushbridger idea?' asked Sir Charles eagerly.

'It is an idea. It suggests – well, it suggests several things, does it not?'

Nobody was quite sure about the several things, but nobody liked to say so, so there was merely an assenting murmur.

Sir Charles took up the tale next. He described his and Egg's visit to Mrs Babbington and its rather negative result.

'And now you're up to date,' he said. 'You know what we do. Tell us: how does it all strike you?'

He leaned forward, boyishly eager.

Poirot was silent for some minutes. The other three watched him.

He said at last:

'Can you remember at all, mademoiselle, what type of port glass Sir Bartholomew had on his table?'

Sir Charles interposed just as Egg was shaking her head vexedly.

'I can tell you that.'

186

He got up and went to a cupboard, where he took out some heavy cut-glass sherry glasses.

'They were a slightly different shape, of course – more rounded – proper port shape. He got them at old Lammersfield's sale – a whole set of table glass. I admired them, and as there were more than he needed, he passed some of them on to me. They're good, aren't they?'

Poirot took the glass and turned it about in his hand.

'Yes,' he said. 'They are fine specimens. I thought something of that kind had been used.'

'Why?' cried Egg.

Poirot merely smiled at her.

'Yes,' he went on, 'the death of Sir Bartholomew Strange could be explained easily enough; but the death of Stephen Babbington is more difficult. Ah, if only it had been the other way about!'

'What do you mean, the other way about?' asked Mr Satterthwaite.

Poirot turned to him.

'Consider, my friend. Sir Bartholomew is a celebrated doctor. There might be many reasons for the death of a celebrated doctor. A doctor knows secrets, my friend, important secrets. A doctor has certain powers. Imagine a patient on the border line of sanity. A word from the doctor, and he will be shut away from the world – what a temptation to an unbalanced brain! A doctor may have suspicions about the sudden death of one of his patients – oh, yes, we can find plenty of motives for the death of a doctor.

'Now, as I say, if only it had been the other way about. If Sir Bartholomew Strange had died *first* and then Stephen Babbington. For Stephen Babbington might have seen something – might have suspected something about the first death.'

He sighed and then resumed.

'But one cannot have a case as one would like to have it. One must take a case as it is. Just one little idea I should like to suggest. I suppose it is not possible that Stephen Babbington's death was an accident – that the poison (if poison there was) was intended for Sir Bartholomew Strange, and that, by mistake, the wrong man was killed.'

'That's an ingenious idea,' said Sir Charles. His face, which had brightened, fell again. 'But I don't believe it will work. Babbington came into this room about four minutes before he was taken ill. During that time the only thing that passed his lips was half a cocktail – there was nothing in that cocktail –'

Poirot interrupted him.

'That you have already told me – but suppose, for the sake of argument, that there was something in that cocktail. Could it have been intended for Sir Bartholomew Strange and did Mr Babbington drink it by mistake?'

Sir Charles shook his head.

'Nobody who knew Tollie at all well would have tried poisoning him in a cocktail.'

'Why?'

'Because he never drank them.'

'Never?'

'Never.'

Poirot made a gesture of annoyance.

'Ah – this business – it goes all wrong. It does not

on Sir Charles, 'I don't see how any
have been mistaken for another – or
kind. Temple carried them round on
one helped themselves to any glass they

murmured Poirot. 'One cannot force a cock-
orces a card. What is she like, this Temple
of yours? She is the maid who admitted me tonight – yes?'

'That's right. I've had her three or four years – nice steady girl – knows her work. I don't know where she came from – Miss Milray would know all about that.'

'Miss Milray, that is your secretary? The tall woman – somewhat of the Grenadier?'

'Very much of the Grenadier,' agreed Sir Charles.

'I have dined with you before on various occasions, but I do not think I met her until that night.'

'No, she doesn't usually dine with us. It was a question of thirteen, you see.'

Sir Charles explained the circumstances, to which Poirot listened very attentively.

'It was her own suggestion that she should be present? I see.'

He remained lost in thought a minute, then he said:

'Might I speak to this parlourmaid of yours, this Temple?'

'Certainly, my dear fellow.'

Sir Charles pressed a bell. It was answered prom

'You rang, sir?'

Temple was a tall girl of thirty-two or three. had a certain smartness – her hair was well bru and glossy, but she was not pretty. Her manner calm and efficient.

'M. Poirot wants to ask you a few questions,' said Sir Charles.

Temple transferred her superior gaze to Poirot.

'We are talking of the night when Mr Babbington died here,' said Poirot. 'You remember that night?'

'Oh, yes, sir.'

'I want to know exactly how cocktails were served.'

'I beg your pardon, sir.'

'I want to know about the cocktails. Did you mix them?'

'No, sir, Sir Charles likes doing that himself. I brought in the bottles – the vermouth, the gin, and all that.'

'Where did you put them?'

'On the table there, sir.'

She indicated a table by the wall.

'The tray with the glasses stood here, sir. Sir Charles, when he had finished mixing and shaking, poured out the cocktails into the glasses. Then I took the tray round and handed it to the ladies and gentlemen.'

'Were all the cocktails on the tray you handed?'

'Sir Charles gave one to Miss Lytton Gore, sir; he was talking to her at the time, and he took his own. And Mr Satterthwaite' – her eyes shifted to him for a moment – 'came and fetched one for a lady – Miss Wills, I think it was.'

'Quite right,' said Mr Satterthwaite.

'The others I handed, sir; I think everyone took one except Sir Bartholomew.'

'Will you be so very obliging, Temple, as to repeat the performance. Let us put cushions for some of the people. I stood here, I remember – Miss Sutcliffe was there.'

Agatha Christie

With Mr Satterthwaite's help, the scene was reconstructed. Mr Satterthwaite was observant. He remembered fairly well where everyone had been in the room. Then Temple did her round. They ascertained that she had started with Mrs Dacres, gone on to Miss Sutcliffe and Poirot, and had then come to Mr Babbington, Lady Mary and Mr Satterthwaite, who had been sitting together.

This agreed with Mr Satterthwaite's recollection.

Finally Temple was dismissed.

'Pah,' cried Poirot. 'It does not make sense. Temple is the last person to handle those cocktails, but it was impossible for her to tamper with them in any way, and, as I say, one cannot force a cocktail on a particular person.'

'It's instinctive to take the one nearest to you,' said Sir Charles.

'Possibly that might work by handing the tray to the person first – but even then it would be very uncertain. The glasses are close together; one does not look particularly nearer than another. No, no, such a haphazard method could not be adopted. Tell me, Mr Satterthwaite, did Mr Babbington put his cocktail down, or did he retain it in his hand?'

'He put it down on this table.'

'Did anyone come near that table after he had done so?'

192

'No. I was the nearest person to him, and I assure you I did not tamper with it in any way – even if I could have done so unobserved.'

Mr Satterthwaite spoke rather stiffly. Poirot hastened to apologize.

'No, no, I am not making an accusation – *quelle idée*! But I want to be very sure of my facts. According to the analysis there was nothing out of the way in that cocktail – now it seems that, apart from that analysis there *could* have been nothing put in it. The same results from two different tests. But Mr Babbington ate or drank nothing else, and if he was poisoned by pure nicotine, death would have resulted very rapidly. You see where that leads us?'

'Nowhere, damn it all,' said Sir Charles.

'I would not say that – no, I would not say that. It suggests a very monstrous idea – which I hope and trust cannot be true. No, of course it is not true – the death of Sir Bartholomew proves that . . . . And yet –'

He frowned, lost in thought. The others watched him curiously. He looked up.

'You see my point, do you not? Mrs Babbington was not at Melfort Abbey, therefore Mrs Babbington is cleared of suspicion.'

'Mrs Babbington – but no one has even dreamed of suspecting her.'

Poirot smiled beneficently.

Agatha Christie

'No? It is a curious thing that. The idea occurred to me at once – but at once. If the poor gentleman is not poisoned by the cocktail, then he must have been poisoned a very few minutes before entering the house. What way could there be? A capsule? Something, perhaps, to prevent indigestion. But who, then, could tamper with that? Only a wife. Who might, perhaps, have a motive that no one outside could possibly suspect? Again a wife.'

'But they were devoted to each other,' cried Egg indignantly. 'You don't understand a bit.'

Poirot smiled kindly at her.

'No. That is valuable. You know, but I do not. I see the facts unbiased by any preconceived notions. And let me tell you something, mademoiselle – in the course of my experience I have known five cases of wives murdered by devoted husbands, and twenty-two of husbands murdered by devoted wives. *Les femmes*, they obviously keep up appearances better.'

'I think you're perfectly horrid,' said Egg. 'I know the Babbingtons are not like that. It's – it's monstrous!'

'Murder is monstrous, mademoiselle,' said Poirot, and there was a sudden sternness in his voice.

He went on in a lighter tone.

'But I – who see only the facts – agree that Mrs Babbington did not do this thing. You see, she was not at Melfort Abbey. No, as Sir Charles has already said, the guilt must lie on a person who was present on both occasions – one of the seven on your list.'

There was a silence.

'And how do you advise us to act?' asked Satterthwaite.

'You have doubtless already your plan?' suggested Poirot.

Sir Charles cleared his throat.

'The only feasible thing seems to be a process of elimination,' he said. 'My idea was to take each person on that list and consider them guilty until they are proved innocent. I mean that we are to feel convinced ourselves that there *is* a connection between that person and Stephen Babbington, and we are to use all our ingenuity to find out what that connection can be. If we find no connection, then we pass on to the next person.'

'It is good psychology, that,' approved Poirot. 'And your methods?'

'That we have not yet had time to discuss. We should welcome your advice on that point, M. Poirot. Perhaps you yourself –'

Poirot held up a hand.

'My friend, do not ask me to do anything of an active nature. It is my lifelong conviction that any problem is best solved by thought. Let me hold what is called, I believe, the watching brief. Continue your investigations which Sir Charles is so ably directing –'

Agatha Christie

'And what about me?' thought Mr Satterthwaite. 'These actors! Always in the limelight playing the star part!'

'You will, perhaps, from time to time require what we may describe as Counsel's opinion. Me, I am the Counsel.'

He smiled at Egg.

'Does that strike you as the sense, mademoiselle?'

'Excellent,' said Egg. 'I'm sure your experience will be very useful to us.'

Her face looked relieved. She glanced at her watch and gave an exclamation.

'I must go home. Mother will have a fit.'

'I'll drive you home,' said Sir Charles.

They went out together.

Chapter 5

Division of Labour

'So you see, the fish has risen,' said Hercule Poirot.

Mr Satterthwaite, who had been looking at the door which had just closed behind the other two, gave a start as he turned to Poirot. The latter was smiling with a hint of mockery.

'Yes, yes, do not deny it. Deliberately you showed me the bait that day in Monte Carlo. Is it not so? You showed me the paragraph in the paper. You hoped that it would arouse my interest – that I should occupy myself with the affair.'

'It is true,' confessed Mr Satterthwaite. 'But I thought that I had failed.'

'No, no, you did not fail. You are a shrewd judge of human nature, my friend. I was suffering from ennui – I had – in the words of the child who was playing near us – "nothing to do". You came at the psychological moment. (And, talking of that, how much crime depends, too, on that psychological moment. The crime, the psychology, they go hand in hand.) But let us come back to our muttons. This is a crime very intriguing – it puzzles me completely.'

'Which crime – the first or the second?'

'There is only one – what you call the first and second murder are only the two halves of the same crime. The second half is simple – the motive – the means adopted –'

Mr Satterthwaite interrupted.

'Surely the means present an equal difficulty. There was no poison found in any of the wine, and the food was eaten by everybody.'

'No, no, it is quite different. In the first case it does not seem as though *anybody* could have poisoned Stephen Babbington. Sir Charles, if he had wanted to, could have poisoned *one* of his guests, but not any particular guest. Temple might possibly have slipped something into the last glass on the tray – but Mr Babbington's was not the last glass. No, the murder of Mr Babbington seems so impossible that I still feel that perhaps it *is* impossible – that he died a natural death after all . . . But that we shall soon know. The second case is different. Any one of the guests present, or the butler or parlourmaid, could have poisoned Bartholomew Strange. That presents no difficulty whatever.'

'I don't see –' began Mr Satterthwaite.

Poirot swept on:

'I will prove that to you some time by a little experiment. Let us pass on to another and most important matter. It is vital, you see (and you *will* see, I am sure, you have the sympathetic heart and the delicate understanding), that I must not play the part of what you call the spoilsport.'

'You mean –' began Mr Satterthwaite with the beginning of a smile.

'That Sir Charles must have the star part! He is used to it. And, moreover, it is expected of him by someone else. Am I not right? It does not please mademoiselle at all that I come to concern myself in this matter.'

'You are what we call "quick in the uptake", M. Poirot.'

'Ah, that, it leaps to the eye! I am of a very susceptible nature – I wish to assist a love affair – not to hinder it. You and I, my friend, must work together in this – to the honour and glory of Charles Cartwright; is it not so? When the case is solved –'

'If –' said Mr Satterthwaite mildly.

'When! I do not permit myself to fail.'

'Never?' asked Mr Satterthwaite searchingly.

'There have been times,' said Poirot with dignity, 'when for a short time, I have been what I suppose you would call slow in the take-up. I have not perceived the truth as soon as I might have done.'

'But you've never failed altogether?'

The persistence of Mr Satterthwaite was curiosity, pure and simple. He wondered . . .

'*Eh bien*,' said Poirot. 'Once. Long ago, in Belgium. We will not talk of it . . .'

'Mr Satterthwaite, his curiosity (and his malice) satisfied, hastened to change the subject.

'Just so. You were saying that when the case is solved –'

'Sir Charles will have solved it. That is essential. I shall have been a little cog in the wheel,' he spread out his hands. 'Now and then, here and there, I shall say a little word – just one little word – a hint, no more. I desire no honour – no renown. I have all the renown I need.'

Mr Satterthwaite studied him with interest. He was amused by the naïve conceit, the immense egoism of the little man. But he did not make the easy mistake of considering it mere empty boasting. An Englishman is usually modest about what he does well, sometimes pleased with himself over something he does badly; but a Latin has a truer appreciation of his own powers. If he is clever he sees no reason for concealing the fact.

'I should like to know,' said Mr Satterthwaite, 'it would interest me very much – just what do you yourself hope to get out of this business? Is it the excitement of the chase?'

Poirot shook his head.

'No – no – it is not that. Like the *chien de chasse*, I follow the scent, and I get excited, and once on the scent I cannot be called off it. All that is true. But there is more . . . It is – how shall I put it? – a passion for getting at the *truth*. In all the world there is nothing so curious and so interesting and so beautiful as truth . . .'

There was silence for a little while after Poirot's words.

Then he took up the paper on which Mr Satterthwaite had carefully copied out the seven names, and read them aloud.

'Mrs Dacres, Captain Dacres, Miss Wills, Miss Sutcliffe, Lady Mary Lytton Gore, Miss Lytton Gore, Oliver Manders.

'Yes,' he said, 'suggestive, is it not?'

'What is suggestive about it?'

'The order in which the names occur.'

'I don't think there is anything suggestive about it. We just wrote the names down without any particular order about it.'

'Exactly. The list is headed by Mrs Dacres. I deduce from that that she is considered the most likely person to have committed the crime.'

'Not the most likely,' said Mr Satterthwaite. 'The least unlikely would express it better.'

'And a third phrase would express it better still. She is perhaps the person you would all *prefer* to have committed the crime.'

Mr Satterthwaite opened his lips impulsively, then met the gentle quizzical gaze of Poirot's shining green eyes, and altered what he had been about to say.

'I wonder – perhaps, M. Poirot, you are right – unconsciously that may be true.'

'I would like to ask you something, Mr Satterthwaite.'

'Certainly – certainly,' Mr Satterthwaite answered complacently.

'From what you have told me, I gather that Sir Charles and Miss Lytton Gore went together to interview Mrs Babbington.'

'Yes.'

'You did not accompany them?'

'No. Three would have been rather a crowd.'

Poirot smiled.

'And also, perhaps, your inclinations led you elsewhere. You had, as they say, different fish to fry. Where did you go, Mr Satterthwaite?'

'I had tea with Lady Mary Lytton Gore,' said Mr Satterthwaite stiffly.

'And what did you talk about?'

'She was so good as to confide in me some of the troubles of her early married life.'

He repeated the substance of Lady Mary's story. Poirot nodded his head sympathetically.

'That is so true to life – the idealistic young girl who marries the bad hat and will listen to nobody. But did you talk of nothing else? Did you, for instance, not speak of Mr Oliver Manders?'

'As a matter of fact we did.'

'And you learnt about him – what?'

Mr Satterthwaite repeated what Lady Mary had told him. Then he said:

'What made you think we had talked of him?'

'Because you went there for that reason. Oh, yes, do not protest. You may *hope* that Mrs Dacres or her husband committed the crime, but you *think* that young Manders did.'

He stilled Mr Satterthwaite's protests.

'Yes, yes, you have the secretive nature. You have your ideas, but you like keeping them to yourself. I have sympathy with you. I do the same myself . . .'

'I don't suspect him – that's absurd. But I just wanted to know more about him.'

'That is as I say. He is your instinctive choice. I, too, am interested in that young man. I was interested in him on the night of the dinner here, because I saw –'

'What did you see?' asked Mr Satterthwaite eagerly.

203

'I saw that there were two people at least (perhaps more) who were playing a part. One was Sir Charles.' He smiled. 'He was playing the naval officer, am I not right? That is quite natural. A great actor does not cease to act because he is not on the stage any more. But young Manders, he too was acting. He was playing the part of the bored and blasé young man – but in reality he was neither bored nor blasé – he was very keenly alive. And therefore, my friend, I noticed him.'

'How did you know I'd been wondering about him?'

'In many little ways. You had been interested in that accident of his that brought him to Melfort Abbey that night. You had not gone with Sir Charles and Miss Lytton Gore to see Mrs Babbington. Why? Because you wanted to follow out some line of your own unobserved. You went to Lady Mary's to find out about someone. Who? It could only be someone local. Oliver Manders. And then, most characteristic, you put his name at the bottom of the list. Who are really the least likely suspects in your mind – Lady Mary and Mademoiselle Egg – but you put his name after theirs, because he is your dark horse, and you want to keep him to yourself.'

'Dear me,' said Mr Satterthwaite. 'Am I really that kind of man?'

'*Précisément.* You have shrewd judgment and observation, and you like keeping its results to yourself. Your opinions of people are your private collection. You do not display them for all the world to see.'

'I believe,' began Mr Satterthwaite, but he was interrupted by the return of Sir Charles.

The actor came in with a springing buoyant step.

'Brrr,' he said. 'It's a wild night.'

He poured himself out a whisky and soda.

Mr Satterthwaite and Poirot both declined.

'Well,' said Sir Charles, 'let's map out our plan of campaign. Where's that list, Satterthwaite? Ah, thanks. Now M. Poirot, Counsel's opinion, if you please. How shall we divide up the spadework?'

'How would you suggest yourself, Sir Charles?'

'Well, we might divide these people up – division of labour – eh? First, there's Mrs Dacres. Egg seems rather keen to take her on. She seems to think that anyone so perfectly turned out won't get impartial treatment from mere males. It seems quite a good idea to approach her through the professional side. Satterthwaite and I might work the other gambit as well if it seemed advisable. Then there's Dacres. I know some of his racing pals. I daresay I could pick up something that way. Then there's Angela Sutcliffe.'

'That also seems to be your work, Cartwright,' said Mr Satterthwaite. 'You know her pretty well, don't you?'

'Yes. That's why I'd rather somebody else tackled

her . . . Firstly,' he smiled ruefully, 'I shall be accused of not putting my back into the job, and secondly – well – she's a friend – you understand?'

'*Parfaitement, parfaitement* – you feel the natural delicacy. It is most understandable. This good Mr Satterthwaite – he will replace you in the task.'

'Lady Mary and Egg – they don't count, of course. What about young Manders? His presence on the night of Tollie's death was an accident; still, I suppose we ought to include him.'

'Mr Satterthwaite will look after young Manders,' said Poirot. 'But I think, Sir Charles, you have missed out a name on your list. You have passed over Miss Muriel Wills.'

'So I have. Well, if Satterthwaite takes on Manders, I'll take on Miss Wills. Is that settled? Any suggestions, M. Poirot?'

'No, no – I do not think so. I shall be interested to hear your results.'

'Of course – that goes without saying. Another idea: If we procured photographs of these people we might use them in making inquiries in Gilling.'

'Excellent,' approved Poirot. 'There was something – ah, yes, your friend, Sir Bartholomew, he did not drink cocktails, but he did drink the port?'

'Yes, he had a particular weakness for port.'

'It seems odd to me that he did not taste anything

unusual. Pure nicotine has a most pungent and unpleasant taste.'

'You've got to remember,' said Sir Charles, 'that there probably wasn't any nicotine in the port. The contents of the glass were analysed, remember.'

'Ah, yes – foolish of me. But, however it was administered – nicotine has a very disagreeable taste.'

'I don't know that that would matter,' said Sir Charles slowly. 'Tollie had a very bad go of influenza last spring, and it left him with his sense of taste and smell a good deal impaired.'

'Ah, yes,' said Poirot thoughtfully. 'That might account for it. That simplifies things considerably.'

Sir Charles went to the window and looked out.

'Still blowing a gale. I'll send for your things, M. Poirot. The Rose and Crown is all very well for enthusiastic artists, but I think you'd prefer proper sanitation and a comfortable bed.'

'You are extremely amiable, Sir Charles.'

'Not at all. I'll see to it now.'

He left the room.

Poirot looked at Mr Satterthwaite.

'If I may permit myself a suggestion.'

'Yes?'

Poirot leaned forward, and said in a low voice:

'*Ask young Manders why he faked an accident.* Tell him the police suspect him – and see what he says.'

207

Chapter 6

Cynthia Dacres

The showrooms of Ambrosine, Ltd, were very pure in appearance. The walls were a shade just off white – the thick pile carpet was so neutral as to be almost colourless – so was the upholstery. Chromium gleamed here and there, and on one wall was a gigantic geometric design in vivid blue and lemon yellow. The room had been designed by Mr Sydney Sandford – the newest and youngest decorator of the moment.

Egg Lytton Gore sat in an arm-chair of modern design – faintly reminiscent of a dentist's chair, and watched exquisite snake-like young women with beautiful bored faces pass sinuously before her. Egg was principally concerned with endeavouring to appear as though fifty or sixty pounds was a mere bagatelle to pay for a dress.

Mrs Dacres, looking as usual marvellously unreal, was (as Egg put it to herself) doing her stuff.

209

'Now, do you like this? Those shoulder knots – rather amusing, don't you think? And the waistline's rather penetrating. I shouldn't have the red lead colour, though – I should have it in the new colour – Espanol – most attractive – like mustard, with a dash of cayenne in it. How do you like Vin Ordinaire? Rather absurd, isn't it? Quite penetrating and ridiculous. Clothes simply must not be serious nowadays.'

'It's very difficult to decide,' said Egg. 'You see' – she became confidential – 'I've never been able to afford any clothes before. We were always so dreadfully poor. I remembered how simply marvellous you looked that night at Crow's Nest, and I thought, "Now that I've got money to spend, I shall go to Mrs Dacres and ask her to advise me." I did admire you so much that night.'

'My dear, how charming of you. I simply adore dressing a young girl. It's so important that girls shouldn't look raw – if you know what I mean.'

'Nothing raw about you,' thought Egg ungratefully. 'Cooked to a turn, you are.'

'You've got so much personality,' continued Mrs Dacres. 'You mustn't have anything at all ordinary. Your clothes must be simple and penetrating – and just faintly visible. You understand? Do you want several things?'

'I thought about four evening frocks, and a couple

no difficulty in inducing her companion to talk freely on the subject of her employer.

'I always think,' said Egg, 'that Mrs Dacres looks a frightful cat. Is she?'

'None of us like her, Miss Lytton Gore, and that's a fact. But she's clever, of course, and she's got a rare head for business. Not like some Society ladies who take up the dressmaking business and go bankrupt because their friends get clothes and don't pay. She's as hard as nails, Madam is – though I will say she's fair enough – and she's got real taste – she knows what's what, and she's clever at getting people to have the style that suits them.'

'I suppose she makes a lot of money?'

A queer knowing look came into Doris's eye.

'It's not for me to say anything – or to gossip.'

'Of course not,' said Egg. 'Go on.'

'But if you ask me – the firm's not far off Queer Street. There was a Jewish gentleman came to see Madam, and there have been one or two things – it's my belief she's been borrowing to keep going in the hope that trade would revive, and that she's got in deep. Really, Miss Lytton Gore, she looks terrible sometimes. Quite desperate. I don't know what she'd look like without her make-up. I don't believe she sleeps of nights.'

'What's her husband like?'

Agatha Christie

'He's a queer fish. Bit of a bad lot, if you ask me. Not that we ever see much of him. None of the other girls agree with me, but I believe she's very keen on him still. Of course a lot of nasty things have been said –'

'Such as?' asked Egg.

'Well, I don't like to repeat things. I never have been one for that.'

'Of course not. Go on, you were saying –?'

'Well, there's been a lot of talk among the girls. About a young fellow – very rich and very soft. Not exactly balmy, if you know what I mean – sort of betwixt and between. Madam's been running him for all she was worth. He might have put things right – he was soft enough for anything – but then he was ordered on a sea voyage – suddenly.'

'Ordered by whom – a doctor?'

'Yes, someone in Harley Street. I believe now that it was the same doctor who was murdered up in Yorkshire – poisoned, so they said.'

'Sir Bartholomew Strange?'

'That was the name. Madam was at the house-party, and we girls said among ourselves – just laughing, you know – well, we said, supposing Madame did him in – out of revenge, you know! Of course it was just *fun* –'

'Naturally,' said Egg. 'Girlish fun. I quite under-stand. You know, Mrs Dacres is quite my idea of a murderess – so hard and remorseless.'

216

'She's ever so hard – and she's got a wicked temper! When she lets go, there's not one of us dares to come near her. They say her husband's frightened of her – and no wonder.'

'Have you ever heard her speak of anyone called Babbington or of a place in Kent – Gilling?'

'Really, now, I can't call to mind that I have.'

Doris looked at her watch and uttered an exclamation.

'Oh, dear, I must hurry. I shall be late.'

'Goodbye, and thanks so much for coming.'

'It's been a pleasure, I'm sure. Goodbye, Miss Lytton Gore, and I hope the article will be a great success. I shall look out for it.'

'You'll look in vain, my girl,' thought Egg, as she asked for her bill.

Then, drawing a line through the supposed jottings for the article, she wrote in her little note-book:

'Cynthia Dacres. Believed to be in financial difficulties. Described as having a "wicked temper". Young man (rich) with whom she was believed to be having an affair was ordered on sea voyage by Sir Bartholomew Strange. Showed no reaction at mention of Gilling or at statement that Babbington knew her.'

'There doesn't seem much there,' said Egg to herself.

Agatha Christie

'A possible motive for the murder of Sir Bartholomew, but very thin. M. Poirot may be able to make something of that. I can't.'

Captain Dacres

Egg had not yet finished her programme for the day. Her next move was to St John's House, in which building the Dacres had a flat. St John's House was a new block of extremely expensive flats. There were sumptuous window-boxes and uniformed porters of such magnificence that they looked like foreign generals.

Egg did not enter the building. She strolled up and down on the opposite side of the street. After about an hour of this she calculated that she must have walked several miles. It was half-past five.

Then a taxi drew up at the Mansions, and Captain Dacres alighted from it. Egg allowed three minutes to elapse, then she crossed the road and entered the building.

Egg pressed the door-bell of No. 3. Dacres himself opened the door. He was still engaged in taking off his overcoat.

219

'Oh,' said Egg. 'How do you do? You do remember me, don't you? We met in Cornwall, and again in Yorkshire.'

'Of course – of course. In at the death both times, weren't we? Come in, Miss Lytton Gore.'

'I wanted to see your wife. Is she in?'

'She's round in Bruton Street – at her dressmaking place.'

'I know. I was there today. I thought perhaps she'd be back by now, and that she wouldn't mind, perhaps, if I came here – only, of course, I suppose I'm being a frightful bother –'

Egg paused appealingly.

Freddie Dacres said to himself:

'Nice looking filly. Damned pretty girl, in fact.'

Aloud he said:

'Cynthia won't be back till well after six. I've just come back from Newbury. Had a rotten day and left early. Come round to the Seventy-Two Club and have a cocktail?'

Egg accepted, though she had a shrewd suspicion that Dacres had already had quite as much alcohol as was good for him.

Sitting in the underground dimness of the Seventy-Two Club, and sipping a Martini, Egg said: 'This is great fun. I've never been here before.'

Freddie Dacres smiled indulgently. He liked a young

and pretty girl. Not perhaps as much as he liked some other things – but well enough.

'Upsettin' sort of time, wasn't it?' he said. 'Up in Yorkshire, I mean. Something rather amusin' about a doctor being poisoned – you see what I mean – wrong way about. A doctor's a chap who poisons other people.'

He laughed uproariously at his own remark and ordered another pink gin.

'That's rather clever of you,' said Egg. 'I never thought of it that way before.'

'Only a joke, of course,' said Freddie Dacres.

'It's odd, isn't it,' said Egg, 'that when we meet it's always at a death.'

'Bit odd,' admitted Captain Dacres. 'You mean the old clergyman chap at what's his name's – the actor fellow's place?'

'Yes. It was very queer the way he died so suddenly.'

'Damn' disturbin',' said Dacres. 'Makes you feel a bit gruey, fellows popping off all over the place. You know, you think "my turn next", and it gives you the shivers.'

'You knew Mr Babbington before, didn't you, at Gilling?'

'Don't know the place. No, I never set eyes on the old chap before. Funny thing is he popped off just the same way as old Strange did. Bit odd, that. Can't have been bumped off, too, I suppose?'

'Well, what do you think?'

Dacres shook his head.

'Can't have been,' he said decisively. 'Nobody murders parsons. Doctors are different.'

'Yes,' said Egg. 'I suppose doctors are different.'

''Course they are. Stands to reason. Doctors are interfering devils.' He slurred the words a little. He leant forward. 'Won't let well alone. Understand?'

'No,' said Egg.

'They monkey about with fellows' lives. They've got a damned sight too much power. Oughtn't to be allowed.'

'I don't quite see what you mean.'

'M' dear girl, I'm *telling* you. Get a fellow shut up – that's what I mean – put him in hell. God, they're cruel. Shut him up and keep the stuff from him – and however much you beg and pray they won't give it you. Don't care a damn what torture you're in. That's doctors for you. I'm telling you – and I *know*.'

His face twitched painfully. His little pinpoint pupils stared past her.

'It's hell, I tell you – hell. And they call it curing you! Pretend they're doing a decent action. Swine!'

'Did Sir Bartholomew Strange –?' began Egg cautiously.

He took the words out of her mouth.

'Sir Bartholomew Strange. Sir Bartholomew Humbug. I'd like to know what goes on in that precious Sanatorium of his. Nerve cases. That's what they say. You're in there and you can't get out. And they say you've gone of your own free will. Free will! Just because they get hold of you when you've got the horrors.'

He was shaking now. His mouth drooped suddenly.

'I'm all to pieces,' he said apologetically. 'All to pieces.' He called to the waiter, pressed Egg to have another drink, and when she refused, ordered one himself.

'That's better,' he said as he drained the glass. 'Got my nerve back now. Nasty business losing your nerve. Mustn't make Cynthia angry. She told me not to talk.' He nodded his head once or twice. 'Wouldn't do to tell the police all this,' he said. 'They might think I'd bumped old Strange off. Eh? You realize, don't you, that someone must have done it? One of us must have killed him. That's a funny thought. Which of us? That's the question.'

'Perhaps *you* know which,' said Egg.

'What d'you say that for? Why should I know?'

He looked at her angrily and suspiciously.

'I don't know anything about it, I tell you. I wasn't going to take that damnable "cure" of his. No matter what Cynthia said – I wasn't going to take it. He was up to something – they were both up to something. But they couldn't fool me.'

He drew himself up.

'I'm a shtrong man, Mish Lytton Gore.'

'I'm sure you are,' said Egg. 'Tell me, do you know anything of a Mrs de Rushbridger who is at the Sanatorium?'

'Rushbridger? Rushbridger? Old Strange said something about her. Now what was it? Can't remember anything.'

He sighed, shook his head.

'Memory's going, that's what it is. And I've got enemies – a lot of enemies. They may be spying on me now.'

He looked round uneasily. Then he leant across the table to Egg.

'What was that woman doing in my room that day?'

'What woman?'

'Rabbit-faced woman. Writes plays. It was the morning after – after he died. I'd just come up from breakfast. She came out of my room and went through the baize door at the end of the passage – went through into the servants' quarters. Odd, eh? Why did she go into my room? What did she think she'd find there? What did she want to go nosing about for, anyway? What's it got to do with her?' He leaned forward confidentially. 'Or do you think it's true what Cynthia says?'

'What does Mrs Dacres say?'

'Says I imagined it. Says I was "seeing things".' He laughed uncertainly. 'I do see things now and again. Pink mice – snakes – all that sort of thing. But seein' a woman's different . . . I *did* see her. She's a queer fish, that woman. Nasty sort of eye she's got. Goes through you.'

He leaned back on the soft couch. He seemed to be dropping asleep.

Egg got up.

'I must be going. Thank you very much, Captain Dacres.'

'Don't thank me. Delighted. Absolutely delighted . . .'
His voice tailed off.

'I'd better go before he passes out altogether,' thought Egg.

She emerged from the smoky atmosphere of the Seventy-Two Club into the cool evening air.

Beatrice, the housemaid, had said that Miss Wills poked and pried. Now came this story from Freddie Dacres. What *had* Miss Wills been looking for? What had she found? Was it possible that Miss Wills *knew* something?

Was there anything in this rather muddled story

about Sir Bartholomew Strange? Had Freddie Dacres secretly feared and hated him?

It seemed possible.

But in all this no hint of any guilty knowledge in the Babbington case.

'How odd it would be,' said Egg to herself, 'if he wasn't murdered after all.'

And then she caught her breath sharply as she caught sight of the words on a newspaper placard a few feet away:

'*CORNISH EXHUMATION CASE – RESULT.*'

Hastily she held out a penny and snatched a paper. As she did so she collided with another woman doing the same thing. As Egg apologized she recognized Sir Charles's secretary, the efficient Miss Milray.

Standing side by side, they both sought the stop-press news. Yes, there it was.

'*RESULT OF CORNISH EXHUMATION.*'

The words danced before Egg's eyes. Analysis of the organs . . . Nicotine . . .

'So he *was* murdered,' said Egg.

'Oh, dear,' said Miss Milray. 'This is terrible – terrible –'

Her rugged countenance was distorted with emotion. Egg looked at her in surprise. She had always regarded Miss Milray as something less than human.

'It upsets me,' said Miss Milray, in explanation. 'You see, I've known him all my life.'

'Mr Babbington?'

'Yes. You see, my mother lives at Gilling, where he used to be vicar. Naturally it's upsetting.'

'Oh, of course.'

'In fact,' said Miss Milray, 'I don't know what to do.'

She flushed a little before Egg's look of astonishment.

'I'd like to write to Mrs Babbington,' she said quickly. 'Only it doesn't seem quite – well, quite . . . I don't know what I had better do about it.'

Somehow, to Egg, the explanation was not quite satisfying.

Chapter 8
Angela Sutcliffe

'Now, are you a friend or are you a sleuth? I simply must know.'

Miss Sutcliffe flashed a pair of mocking eyes as she spoke. She was sitting in a straight-backed chair, her grey hair becomingly arranged, her legs were crossed and Mr Satterthwaite admired the perfection of her beautifully shod feet and her slender ankles. Miss Sutcliffe was a very fascinating woman, mainly owing to the fact that she seldom took anything seriously.

'Is that quite fair?' asked Mr Satterthwaite.

'My dear man, of course it's fair. Have you come here for the sake of my beautiful eyes, as the French say so charmingly, or have you, you nasty man, come just to pump me about murders?'

'Can you doubt that your first alternative is the correct one?' asked Mr Satterthwaite with a little bow.

'I can and I do,' said the actress with energy. 'You

are one of those people who look so mild, and really wallow in blood.'

'No, no.'

'Yes, yes. The only thing I can't make up my mind about is whether it is an insult or a compliment to be considered a potential murderess. On the whole, I think it's a compliment.'

She cocked her head a little on one side and smiled that slow bewitching smile that never failed.

Mr Satterthwaite thought to himself:

'Adorable creature.'

Aloud he said, 'I will admit, dear lady, that the death of Sir Bartholomew Strange has interested me considerably. I have, as you perhaps know, dabbled in such doings before . . .'

He paused modestly, perhaps hoping that Miss Sutcliffe would show some knowledge of his activities. However, she merely asked:

'Tell me one thing – is there anything in what that girl said?'

'Which girl, and what did she say?'

'The Lytton Gore girl. The one who is so fascinated by Charles. (What a wretch Charles is – he will do it!) She thinks that that nice old man down in Cornwall was murdered, too.'

'What do you think?'

'Well, it certainly happened just the same way . . .

She's an intelligent girl, you know. Tell me – is Charles serious?'

'I expect your views on the subject are likely to be much more valuable than mine,' said Mr Satterthwaite.

'What a tiresomely discreet man you are,' cried Miss Sutcliffe. 'Now I' – she sighed – 'am appallingly indiscreet . . .'

She fluttered an eyelash at him.

'I know Charles pretty well. I know men pretty well. He seems to me to display all the signs of settling down. There's an air of virtue about him. He'll be handing round the plate and founding a family in record time – that's my view. How dull men are when they decide to settle down! They lose all their charm.'

'I've often wondered why Sir Charles has never married,' said Mr Satterthwaite.

'My dear, he never showed any signs of wanting to marry. He wasn't what they call a marrying man. But he was a very attractive man . . .' She sighed. A slight twinkle showed in her eyes as she looked at Mr Satterthwaite. 'He and I were once – well, why deny what everybody knows? It was very pleasant while it lasted . . . and we're still the best of friends. I suppose that's the reason the Lytton Gore child looks at me so fiercely. She suspects I still have a *tendresse* for Charles. Have I? Perhaps I have. But at any rate I haven't yet written my memoirs describing all my

231

affairs in detail as most of my friends seem to have done. If I did, you know, the girl wouldn't like it. She'd be shocked. Modern girls are easily shocked. Her mother wouldn't be shocked at all. You can't really shock a sweet mid-Victorian. They say so little, but always think the worst . . .'

Mr Satterthwaite contented himself with saying:

'I think you are right in suspecting that Egg Lytton Gore mistrusts you.'

Miss Sutcliffe frowned.

'I'm not at all sure that I'm not a little jealous of her . . . we women are such cats, aren't we? Scratch, scratch, miauw, miauw, purr, purr . . .'

She laughed.

'Why didn't Charles come and catechize me on this business? Too much nice feeling, I suppose. The man must think me guilty . . . Am I guilty, Mr Satterthwaite? What do you think now?'

She stood up and stretched out a hand.

'All the perfumes of Arabia will not sweeten this little hand –'

She broke off.

'No, I'm not Lady Macbeth. Comedy's my line.'

'There seems also a certain lack of motive,' said Mr Satterthwaite.

'True. I liked Bartholomew Strange. We were friends. I had no reason for wishing him out of the way. Because we were friends I'd rather like to take an active part in hunting down his murderer. Tell me if I can help in any way.'

'I suppose, Miss Sutcliffe, you didn't see or hear anything that might have a bearing on the crime?'

'Nothing that I haven't already told the police. The house-party had only just arrived, you know. His death occurred on that first evening.'

'The butler?'

'I hardly noticed him.'

'Any peculiar behaviour on the part of the guests?'

'No. Of course that boy – what's his name? Manders turned up rather unexpectedly.'

'Did Sir Bartholomew Strange seemed surprised?'

'Yes, I think he was. He said to me just before we went in to dinner that it was an odd buisness, "a new method of gate crashing", he called it. "Only," he said, "it's my wall he's crashed, not my gate."'

'Sir Bartholomew was in good spirits?'

'Very good spirits!'

'What about this secret passage you mentioned to the police?'

'I believe it led out of the library. Sir Bartholomew promised to show it to me – but of course the poor man died.'

'How did the subject come up?'

'We were discussing a recent purchase of his – an old

walnut bureau. I asked if it had a secret drawer in it. I told him I adored secret drawers. It's a secret passion of mine. And he said, "No, there wasn't a secret drawer that he knew of – but he had got a secret passage in the house."'

'He didn't mention a patient of his, a Mrs de Rushbridger?'

'No.'

'Do you know a place called Gilling, in Kent?'

'Gilling? Gilling, no, I don't think I do. Why?'

'Well, you knew Mr Babbington before, didn't you?'

'Who is Mr Babbington?'

'The man who died, or who was killed, at the Crow's Nest.'

'Oh, the clergyman. I'd forgotten his name. No, I'd never seen him before in my life. Who told you I knew him?'

'Someone who ought to know,' said Mr Satterthwaite boldly.

Miss Sutcliffe seemed amused.

'Dear old man, did they think I'd had an affair with him? Archdeacons are sometimes very naughty, aren't they? So why not vicars? There's the man in the barrel, isn't there? But I must clear the poor man's memory. I'd never seen him before in my life.'

And with that statement Mr Satterthwaite was forced to rest content.

Chapter 9
Muriel Wills

Five Upper Cathcart Road, Tooting, seemed an incongruous home for a satiric playwright. The room into which Sir Charles was shown had walls of a rather drab oatmeal colour with a frieze of laburnum round the top. The curtains were of rose-coloured velvet, there were a lot of photographs and china dogs, the telephone was coyly hidden by a lady with ruffled skirts, there were a great many little tables and some suspicious-looking brasswork from Birmingham via the Far East.

Miss Wills entered the room so noiselessly that Sir Charles, who was at the moment examining a ridiculously elongated pierrot doll lying across the sofa, did not hear her. Her thin voice saying, 'How d'you do, Sir Charles. This is really a great pleasure,' made him spin round.

Miss Wills was dressed in a limp jumper suit which hung disconsolately on her angular form. Her stockings were slightly wrinkled, and she had on very high-heeled patent leather slippers.

Sir Charles shook hands, accepted a cigarette, and sat down on the sofa by the pierrot doll. Miss Wills sat opposite him. The light from the window caught her pince-nez and made them give off little flashes.

'Fancy you finding me out here,' said Miss Wills. 'My mother will be ever so excited. She just adores the theatre – especially anything romantic. That play where you were a Prince at a University – she's often talked of it. She goes to matinées, you know, and eats chocolates – she's one of that kind. And she does love it.'

'How delightful,' said Sir Charles. 'You don't know how charming it is to be remembered. The public memory is short!' He sighed.

'She'll be thrilled at meeting you,' said Miss Wills. 'Miss Sutcliffe came the other day, and Mother was thrilled at meeting her.'

'Angela was here?'

'Yes. She's putting on a play of mine, you know: *Little Dog Laughed*.'

'Of course,' said Sir Charles. 'I've read about it. Rather intriguing title.'

'I'm so glad you think so. Miss Sutcliffe likes it, too. It's a kind of modern version of the nursery rhyme – a lot of froth and nonsense – Hey diddle diddle and the dish and the spoon scandal. Of course, it all revolves round Miss Sutcliffe's part – everyone dances to her fiddling – that's the idea.'

Sir Charles said:

'Not bad. The world nowadays is rather like a mad nursery rhyme. And the little dog laughed to see such sport, eh?' And he thought suddenly: 'Of course this woman's the Little Dog. She looks on and laughs.'

The light shifted from Miss Will's pince-nez, and he saw her pale-blue eyes regarding him intelligently through them.

'This woman,' thought Sir Charles, 'has a fiendish sense of humour.'

Aloud he said:

'I wonder if you can guess what errand has brought me here?'

'Well,' said Miss Wills archly, 'I don't suppose it was only to see poor little me.'

Sir Charles registered for a moment the difference between the spoken and the written word. On paper Miss Wills was witty and cynical, in speech she was arch.

'It was really Satterthwaite put the idea into my head,' said Sir Charles. 'He fancies himself as being a good judge of character.'

'He's very clever about people,' said Miss Wills. 'It's rather his hobby, I should say.'

'And he is strongly of opinion that if there were

anything worth noticing that night at Melfort Abbey you would have noticed it.'

'Is that what he said?'

'Yes.'

'I was very interested, I must admit,' said Miss Wills slowly. 'You see, I'd never seen a murder at close hand before. A writer's got to take everything as copy, hasn't she?'

'I believe that's a well-known axiom.'

'So naturally,' said Miss Wills, 'I tried to notice everything I could.'

This was obviously Miss Will's version of Beatrice's 'poking and prying.'

'About the guests?'

'About the guests.'

'And what exactly did you notice?'

The pince-nez shifted.

'I didn't really find out anything – if I had I'd have told the police, of course,' she added virtuously.

'But you noticed things.'

'I always do notice things. I can't help it. I'm funny that way.' She giggled.

'And you noticed – what?'

'Oh, nothing – that is – nothing that you'd call anything, Sir Charles. Just little odds and ends about people's characters. I find people so very interesting. So typical, if you know what I mean.'

'Typical of what?'

'Of themselves. Oh, I can't explain. I'm ever so silly at saying things.'

She giggled again.

'Your pen is deadlier than your tongue,' said Sir Charles, smiling.

'I don't think it's very nice of you to say deadlier, Sir Charles.'

'My dear Miss Wills, admit that with a pen in your hand you're quite merciless.'

'I think you're horrid, Sir Charles. It's *you* who are merciless to *me*.'

'I must get out of this bog of badinage,' said Sir Charles to himself. He said aloud:

'So you didn't find out anything concrete, Miss Wills?'

'No – not exactly. At least, there was one thing. Something I noticed and ought to have told the police about, only I forgot.'

'What was that?'

'The butler. He had a kind of strawberry mark on his left wrist. I noticed it when he was handing me vegetables. I suppose that's the sort of thing which might come in useful.'

'I should say very useful indeed. The police are trying hard to track down that man Ellis. Really, Miss Wills, you are a very remarkable woman. Not one of the servants or guests mentioned such a mark.'

'Most people don't use their eyes much, do they?' said Miss Wills.

'Where exactly was the mark? And what size was it?'

'If you'll just stretch out your own wrist –' Sir Charles extended his arm. 'Thank you. It was here.' Miss Wills placed an unerring finger on the spot. 'It was about the size, roughly, of a sixpence, and rather the shape of Australia.'

'Thank you, that's very clear,' said Sir Charles, removing his hand and pulling down his cuffs again.

'You think I ought to write to the police and tell them?'

'Certainly I do. It might be most valuable in tracing the man. Dash it all,' went on Sir Charles with feeling, 'in detective stories there's always some identifying mark on the villain. I thought it was a bit hard that real life should prove so lamentably behindhand.'

'It's usually a scar in stories,' said Miss Wills thoughtfully.

'A birthmark's just as good,' said Sir Charles.

He looked boyishly pleased.

'The trouble is,' he went on, 'most people are so indeterminate. There's nothing about them to take hold of.'

Miss Wills looked inquiringly at him.

'Old Babbington, for instance,' went on Sir Charles,

'he had a curiously vague personality. Very difficult to lay hold of.'

'His hands were very characteristic,' said Miss Wills. 'What I call a scholar's hands. A little crippled with arthritis, but very refined fingers and beautiful nails.'

'What an observer you are. Ah, but – of course, you knew him before.'

'Knew Mr Babbington?'

'Yes, I remember his telling me so – where was it he said he had known you?'

Miss Wills shook her head decisively.

'Not me. You must have been mixing me up with someone else – or he was. I'd never met him before.'

'It must be a mistake. I thought – at Gilling –'

He looked at her keenly. Miss Wills appeared quite composed.

'No,' she said.

'Did it ever occur to you, Miss Wills, that he might have been murdered, too?'

'I know you and Miss Lytton Gore think so – or rather *you* think so.'

'Oh – and – er – what do *you* think?'

'It doesn't seem likely,' said Miss Wills.

A little baffled by Miss Wills's clear lack of interest in the subject Sir Charles started on another tack.

'Did Sir Bartholomew mention a Mrs de Rushbridger at all?'

Agatha Christie

'No, I don't think so.'

'She was a patient in his Home. Suffering from nervous breakdown and loss of memory.'

'He mentioned a case of lost memory,' said Miss Wills. 'He said you could hypnotize a person and bring their memory back.'

'Did he, now? I wonder – could that be significant?'

Sir Charles frowned and remained lost in thought. Miss Wills said nothing.

'There's nothing else you could tell me? Nothing about any of the guests?'

It seemed to him there was just the slightest pause before Miss Wills answered.

'No.'

'About Mrs Dacres? Or Captain Dacres? Or Miss Sutcliffe? Or Mr Manders?'

He watched her very intently as he pronounced each name.

Once he thought he saw the pince-nez flicker, but he could not be sure.

'I'm afraid there's nothing I can tell you, Sir Charles.'

'Oh, well!' He stood up. 'Satterthwaite will be disappointed.'

'I'm so sorry,' said Miss Wills primly.

'I'm sorry, too, for disturbing you. I expect you were busy writing.'

'I was, as a matter of fact.'

'Another play?'

'Yes. To tell you the truth, I thought of using some of the characters at the house-party at Melfort Abbey.'

'What about libel?'

'That's quite all right, Sir Charles, I find people never recognize themselves.' She giggled. 'Not if, as you said just now, one is really merciless.'

'You mean,' said Sir Charles, 'that we all have an exaggerated idea of our own personalities and don't recognize the truth if it's sufficiently brutally portrayed. I was quite right, Miss Wills, you *are* a cruel woman.'

Miss Wills tittered.

'You needn't be afraid, Sir Charles. Women aren't usually cruel to men – unless it's some particular man – they're only cruel to other women.'

'Meaning you've got your analytical knife into some unfortunate female. Which one? Well, perhaps I can guess. Cynthia's not beloved by her own sex.'

Miss Wills said nothing. She continued to smile – rather a catlike smile.

'Do you write your stuff or dictate it?'

'Oh, I write it and send it to be typed.'

'You ought to have a secretary.'

'Perhaps. Have you still got that clever Miss – Miss Milray, wasn't it?'

243

'Yes, I've got Miss Milray. She went away for a time to look after her mother in the country, but she's back again now. Most efficient woman.'

'So I should think. Perhaps a little impulsive.'

'Impulsive? Miss Milray?'

Sir Charles stared. Never in his wildest flights of fancy had he associated impulse with Miss Milray.

'Only on occasions, perhaps,' said Miss Wills.

Sir Charles shook his head.

'Miss Milray's the perfect robot. Goodbye, Miss Wills. Forgive me for bothering you, and don't forget to let the police know about that thingummybob.'

'The mark on the butler's right wrist? No, I won't forget.'

'Well, goodbye – half a sec. – did you say right wrist? You said left just now.'

'Did I? How stupid of me.'

'Well, which was it?'

Miss Wills frowned and half closed her eyes.

'Let me see. I was sitting so – and he – would you mind, Sir Charles, handing me that brass plate as though it was a vegetable dish. Left side.'

Sir Charles presented the beaten brass atrocity as directed.

'Cabbage, madam?'

'Thank you,' said Miss Wills, 'I'm quite sure now. It was the left wrist, as I said first. Stupid of me.'

'No, no,' said Sir Charles. 'Left and right are always puzzling.'

He said goodbye for the third time.

As he closed the door he looked back. Miss Wills was not looking at him. She was standing where he had left her. She was gazing at the fire, and on her lips was a smile of satisfied malice.

Sir Charles was startled.

'That woman knows something,' he said to himself. 'I'll swear she knows something. And she won't say . . . But what the devil is it she knows?'

Chapter 10
Oliver Manders

At the office of Messrs Speier & Ross, Mr Satterthwaite asked for Mr Oliver Manders and sent in his card.

Presently he was ushered into a small room, where Oliver was sitting at a writing-table.

The young man got up and shook hands.

'Good of you to look me up, sir,' he said.

His tone implied:

'I have to say that, but really it's a damned bore.'

Mr Satterthwaite, however, was not easily put off. He sat down, blew his nose thoughtfully, and, peering over the top of his handkerchief, said:

'Seen the news this morning?'

'You mean the new financial situation? Well, the dollar –'

'Not dollars,' said Mr Satterthwaite. 'Death. The result of the Loomouth exhumation. Babbington was poisoned – by nicotine.'

'Oh, that – yes, I saw that. Our energetic Egg will be pleased. She always insisted it was murder.'

'But it doesn't interest you?'

'My tastes aren't so crude. After all, murder –' he shrugged his shoulders. 'So violent and inartistic.'

'Not always inartistic,' said Mr Satterthwaite.

'No? Well, perhaps not.'

'It depends, does it not, on who commits the murder. You, for instance, would, I am sure, commit a murder in a very artistic manner.'

'Nice of you to say so,' drawled Oliver.

'But frankly, my dear boy, I don't think much of the accident you faked. No more do the police, I understand.'

There was a moment's silence – then a pen dropped to the floor.

Oliver said:

'Excuse me, I don't quite understand you.'

'That rather inartistic performance of yours at Melfort Abbey. I *should* be interested to know – just why you did it.'

There was another silence, then Oliver said:

'You say the police – suspect?'

Mr Satterthwaite nodded.

'It looks a little suspicious, don't you think?' he asked pleasantly. 'But perhaps you have a perfectly good explanation.'

248

'I've got an explanation,' said Oliver slowly. 'Whether it's a good one or not, I don't know.'

'Will you let me judge?'

There was a pause, then Oliver said:

'I came there – the way I did – at Sir Bartholomew's own suggestion.'

'What?' Mr Satterthwaite was astonished.

'A bit odd, isn't it? But it's true. I got a letter from him suggesting that I should have a sham accident and claim hospitality. He said he couldn't put his reasons in writing, but he would explain them to me at the first opportunity.'

'And did he explain?'

'No, he didn't . . . I got there just before dinner. I didn't see him alone. At the end of dinner he – he died.'

The weariness had gone out of Oliver's manner. His dark eyes were fixed on Mr Satterthwaite. He seemed to be studying attentively the reactions aroused by his words.

'You've got this letter?'

'No, I tore it up.'

'A pity,' said Mr Satterthwaite dryly. 'And you said nothing to the police?'

'No, it all seemed – well, rather fantastic.'

'It is fantastic.'

Mr Satterthwaite shook his head. Had Bartholomew

Strange written such a letter? It seemed highly uncharacteristic. The story had a melodramatic touch most unlike the physician's cheerful common sense.

He looked up at the young man. Oliver was still watching him. Mr Satterthwaite thought: 'He's looking to see if I swallow this story.'

He said, 'And Sir Bartholomew gave absolutely no reason for his request?'

'None whatever.'

'An extraordinary story.'

Oliver did not speak.

'Yet you obeyed the summons?'

Something of the weary manner returned.

'Yes, it seemed refreshingly out of the way to a somewhat jaded palate. I was curious, I must confess.'

'Is there anything else?' asked Mr Satterthwaite.

'What do you mean, sir, anything else?'

Mr Satterthwaite did not really know what he meant. He was led by some obscure instinct.

'I mean,' he said, 'is there anything else that might tell – against you?'

There was a pause. Then the young man shrugged his shoulders.

'I suppose I might as well make a clean breast of it. The woman isn't likely to hold her tongue about it.'

Mr Satterthwaite looked a question.

'It was the morning after the murder stuff. I was

250

talking to the Anthony Armstrong woman. I took out my pocket-book and something fell out of it. She picked it up and handed it back to me.'

'And this something?'

'Unfortunately she glanced at it before returning it to me. It was a cutting from a newspaper about nicotine – what a deadly poison it was, and so on.'

'How did you come to have such an interest in the subject?'

'I didn't. I suppose I must have put that cutting in my wallet sometime or other, but I can't remember doing so. Bit awkward, eh?'

Mr Satterthwaite thought: 'A thin story.'

'I suppose,' went on Oliver Manders, 'she went to the police about it?'

Mr Satterthwaite shook his head.

'I don't think so. I fancy she's a woman who likes – well, to keep things to herself. She's a collector of knowledge.'

Oliver Manders leaned forward suddenly.

'I'm innocent, sir, absolutely innocent.'

'I haven't suggested that you are guilty,' said Mr Satterthwaite mildly.

'But someone has – someone must have done. Someone has put the police on to me.'

Mr Satterthwaite shook his head.

'No, no.'

Agatha Christie

'Then why did you come here today?'

'Partly as the result of my – er – investigations on the spot.' Mr Satterthwaite spoke a little pompously. 'And partly at the suggestion of – a friend.'

'What friend?'

'Hercule Poirot.'

'That man!' The expression burst from Oliver. 'Is he back in England?'

'Yes.'

'Why has he come back?'

Mr Satterthwaite rose.

'Why does a dog go hunting?' he inquired.

And, rather pleased with his retort, he left the room.

Chapter 11

Poirot Gives A Sherry Party

I

Sitting in a comfortable arm-chair in his slightly florid suite at the Ritz, Hercule Poirot listened.

Egg was perched on the arm of a chair, Sir Charles stood in front of the fireplace, Mr Satterthwaite sat a little farther away observing the group.

'It's failure all along the line,' said Egg.

'Poirot shook his head gently.

'No, no, you exaggerate. As regards a link with Mr Babbington, you have drawn the blank – yes; but you have collected other suggestive information.'

'The Wills woman knows something,' said Sir Charles. 'I'll swear she knows something.'

'And Captain Dacres, he too has not the clear conscience. And Mrs Dacres was desperately in want of money, and Sir Bartholomew spoilt her chance of laying hold of some.'

'What do you think of young Manders's story?' asked Mr Satterthwaite.

Agatha Christie

'It strikes me as peculiar and as being highly uncharacteristic of the late Sir Bartholomew Strange.'

'You mean it's a lie?' asked Sir Charles bluntly.

'There are so many kinds of lies,' said Hercule Poirot.

He was silent for a minute or two, then he said:

'This Miss Wills, she has written a play for Miss Sutcliffe?'

'Yes. The first night is Wednesday next.'

'Ah!'

He was silent again. Egg said:

'Tell us: What shall we do now?'

The little man smiled at her.

'There is only one thing to do – think.'

'Think?' cried Egg. Her voice was disgusted.

Poirot beamed on her.

'But yes, exactly that. *Think*! With thought, all problems can be solved.'

'Can't we do something?'

'For you the action, eh, mademoiselle? But certainly, there are still things you can do. There is, for instance, this place, Gilling, where Mr Babbington lived for so many years. You can make inquiries there. You say that this Miss Milray's mother lives at Gilling and is an invalid. An invalid knows everything. She hears everything and forgets nothing. Make your inquiries of her, it may lead to something – who knows?'

'Aren't *you* going to do anything?' demanded Egg persistently.

Poirot twinkled.

'You insist that I, too, shall be active? *Eh bien*. It shall be as you wish. Only me, I shall not leave this place. I am very comfortable here. But I will tell you what I will do: I will give the party – the Sherry Party – that is fashionable, is it not?'

'A Sherry Party?'

'*Précisément,* and to it I will ask Mrs Dacres, Captain Dacres, Miss Sutcliffe, Miss Wills, Mr Manders and your charming mother, mademoiselle.'

'And me?'

'Naturally, and you. The present company is included.'

'Hurrah,' said Egg. 'You can't deceive me, M. Poirot. Something will happen at that party. It will, won't it?'

'We shall see,' said Poirot. 'But do not expect too much, mademoiselle. Now leave me with Sir Charles, for there are a few things about which I want to ask his advice.'

As Egg and Mr Satterthwaite stood waiting for the lift, Egg said ecstatically:

'It's lovely – just like detective stories. All the people will be there, and then he'll tell us *which* of them did it.'

'I wonder,' said Mr Satterthwaite.

Agatha Christie

II

The Sherry Party took place on Monday evening. The invitation had been accepted by all. The charming and indiscreet Miss Sutcliffe laughed mischievously as she glanced round.

'Quite the spider's parlour, M. Poirot. And here all we poor little flies have walked in. I'm sure you're going to give us the most marvellous résumé of the case and then suddenly you'll point at me and say, "Thou art the woman", and everyone will say, "She done it", and I shall burst into tears and confess because I'm too terribly suggestible for words. Oh, M. Poirot, I'm so frightened of you.'

'*Quelle histoire*,' cried Poirot. He was busy with a decanter and glasses. He handed her a glass of sherry with a bow. 'This is a friendly little party. Do not let us talk of murders and bloodshed and poison. *Là, là!* these things, they spoil the palate.'

He handed a glass to the grim Miss Milray, who had accompanied Sir Charles and was standing with a forbidding expression on her face.

'*Voilà*,' said Poirot as he finished dispensing hospitality. 'Let us forget the occasion on which we first met. Let us have the party spirit. Eat, drink and be merry, for tomorrow we die. *Ah, malheur*, I have again mentioned death. Madame,' he bowed to Mrs Dacres, 'may I be permitted to wish you good luck and congratulate you on your very charming gown.'

'Here's to you, Egg,' said Sir Charles.

'Cheerio,' said Freddie Dacres.

Everybody murmured something. There was an air of forced gaiety about the proceedings. Everyone was determine to appear gay and unconcerned. Only Poirot himself seemed naturally so. He rambled on happily . . .

'The sherry, I prefer it to the cocktail – and a thousand times to the whisky. Ah, *quel horreur*, the whisky. By drinking the whisky, you ruin, absolutely ruin, the palate. The delicate wines of France, to appreciate them, you must never never – ah *qu'est-ce qu'il y a* –?'

A strange sound had interrupted him – a kind of choking cry. Every eye went to Sir Charles as he stood swaying, his face convulsed. The glass dropped from his hand on to the carpet, he took a few steps blindly, then collapsed.

There was a moment's stupefied silence, then Angela Sutcliffe screamed and Egg started forward.

'Charles,' cried Egg. 'Charles.'

She fought her way blindly forward. Mr Satterthwaite gently held her back.

'Oh, dear God,' cried Lady Mary. '*Not another!*'

257

Angela Sutcliffe cried out:

'He's been poisoned, too . . . . This is awful. Oh, my God, this is too awful . . .'

And suddenly collapsing on to a sofa, she began to sob and laugh – a horrible sound.

Poirot had taken charge of the situation. He was kneeling by the prostrate man. The others drew back while he made his examination. He rose to his feet, mechanically dusting the knees of his trousers. He looked round at the assembly. There was complete silence, except for the smothered sobs of Angela Sutcliffe.

'My friends,' began Poirot.

He got no further, for Egg spat out at him:

'You fool. You absurd play-acting little fool! Pretending to be so great and so wonderful, and to know all about everything. And now you let this happen. Another murder. Under your very nose . . . If you'd let the whole thing alone this wouldn't have happened . . . It's you who have murdered Charles – you – you – you . . .'

She stopped, unable to get out the words.

Poirot nodded his head gravely and sadly.

'It is true, mademoiselle. I confess it. It is I who have murdered Sir Charles. But I, mademoiselle, am a very special kind of murderer. I can kill – and I can restore to life.' He turned and in a different tone of voice, an apologetic everyday voice, he said:

'A magnificent performance, Sir Charles, I congratulate you. Perhaps you would now like to take your curtain.'

With a laugh the actor sprang to his feet and bowed mockingly.

Egg gave a great gasp.

'M. Poirot, you – you *beast*.'

'Charles,' cried Angela Sutcliffe. 'You complete devil . . .'

'But why –?'

'How –?'

'What on earth –?'

By means of his upraised hand, Poirot obtained silence.

'Messieurs, mesdames. I demand pardon of you all. This little farce was necessary to prove to you all, and incidentally, to prove to myself a fact which my reason already told me is true.

'Listen. On this tray of glasses I placed in one glass a teaspoonful of plain water. That water represented pure nicotine. These glasses are of the same kind as those possessed by Sir Charles Cartwright and by Sir Bartholomew Strange. Owing to the heavy cut glass, a small quantity of a colourless liquid is quite undetectable. Imagine, then, the port glass of Sir Bartholomew Strange. After it was put on the table somebody introduced into it a sufficient quantity of pure nicotine. That might have been done by anybody. The butler, the parlour-maid, or one of the guests who slipped into the dining-room on his or her way downstairs. Dessert arrived, the port is taken round, the glass is filled. Sir Bartholomew drinks – and dies.

'Tonight we have played a third tragedy – a sham tragedy – I asked Sir Charles to play the part of the victim. This he did magnificently. Now suppose for a minute that this was not a farce, but truth. *Sir Charles is dead.* What will be the steps taken by the police?'

Miss Sutcliffe cried:

'Why, the glass, of course.' She nodded to where the glass lay on the floor as it had fallen from Sir Charles's hand. 'You only put water in, but if it had been nicotine –'

'Let us suppose it was nicotine.' Poirot touched the glass gently with his toe. 'You are of opinion that the police would analyse the glass, and that traces of nicotine would be found?'

'Certainly.'

Poirot shook his head gently.

'You are wrong. No nicotine would be found.'

They stared at him.

'You see,' he smiled, '*that* is not the glass from which Sir Charles drank.' With an apologetic grin he extended a glass from the tail pocket of his coat. '*This* is the glass he used.'

He went on:

'It is, you see, the simple theory of the conjuring trick. The attention cannot be in two places at once. To do my conjuring trick I need the attention focused elsewhere. Well, there is a moment, a psychological moment. When Sir Charles falls – dead – every eye in the room is on his dead body. Everyone crowds forward to get near him, and no one, no one at all, looks at Hercule Poirot, and in that moment I exchange the glasses and no one sees . . .

'So you see, I prove my point . . . There was such a moment at Crow's Nest, there was such a moment at Melfort Abbey – and so, there was nothing in the cocktail glass and nothing in the port glass . . .'

Egg cried:

'Who changed them?'

Looking at her, Poirot replied:

'That, we have still to find out . . .'

'You don't know?'

Poirot shrugged his shoulders.

Rather uncertainly, the guests made signs of departure. Their manner was a little cold. They felt they had been badly fooled.

With a gesture of the hand, Poirot arrested them.

'One little moment, I pray of you. There is one thing more that I have to say. Tonight, admittedly, we have played the comedy. But the comedy may be played in earnest – it may become a tragedy. Under certain conditions the murderer may strike a third time . . . I speak now to all of you here present. *If anyone of you knows something – something that may bear in any way on this crime, I implore that person to speak now.* To keep knowledge to oneself at this juncture may be dangerous – so dangerous that death may be the result of silence. Therefore I beg again – *if anyone knows anything, let that person speak now . . .'*

It seemed to Sir Charles that Poirot's appeal was addressed especially to Miss Wills. If so, it had no result. Nobody spoke or answered.

Poirot sighed. His hand fell.

'Be it so, then. I have given warning. I can do no more. Remember, to keep silence is dangerous . . .'

But still nobody spoke.

Awkwardly the guests departed.

Egg, Sir Charles and Mr Satterthwaite were left.

Egg had not yet forgiven Poirot. She sat very still, her cheeks flushed and her eyes angry. She wouldn't look at Sir Charles.

'That was a damned clever bit of work, Poirot,' said Sir Charles appreciatively.

'Amazing,' said Mr Satterthwaite with a chuckle. 'I wouldn't have believed that I wouldn't have seen you do that exchange.'

'That is why,' said Poirot, 'I could take no one into

any confidence. The experiment could only be fair this way.'

'Was that the only reason you planned this – to see whether it could be done unnoticed?'

'Well, not quite, perhaps. I had one other aim.'

'Yes?'

'I wanted to watch the expression on one person's face when Sir Charles fell dead.'

'Which person's?' said Egg sharply.

'Ah, that is my secret.'

'And you did watch that person's face?' asked Mr Satterthwaite.

'Yes.'

'Well?'

Poirot did not reply. He merely shook his head.

'Won't you tell us what you saw there?'

Poirot said slowly:

'I saw an expression of the utmost surprise . . .'

Egg drew her breath in sharply.

'You mean,' she said, '*that you know who the murderer is?*'

'You can put it that way if you like, mademoiselle.'

'But then – but then – you know everything?'

Poirot shook his head.

'No; on the contrary I know nothing at all. For, you see, I do not know *why* Stephen Babbington was killed. Until I know that I can prove nothing, I can know nothing . . . It all hinges on that – the motive for Stephen Babbington's death . . .'

There was a knock at the door and a page entered with a telegram on a tray.

Poirot opened it. His face changed. He handed the telegram to Sir Charles. Leaning over Sir Charles's shoulder, Egg read it aloud:

> *'Please come and see me at once can give you valuable information as to Bartholomew Strange's death – Margaret Rushbridger.'*

'Mrs de Rushbridger!' cried Sir Charles. 'We were right after all. She *has* got something to do with the case.'

Chapter 12

Day At Gilling

I

At once an excited discussion sprang up. An A.B.C. was produced. It was decided that an early train would be better than going by car.

'At last,' said Sir Charles, 'we're going to get that particular part of the mystery cleared up.'

'What do you think the mystery is?' asked Egg.

'I can't imagine. But it can't fail to throw some light on the Babbington affair. If Tollie got those people together on purpose, as I feel pretty sure he did, then the "surprise" he talked of springing on them had something to do with this Rushbridger woman. I think we can assume that, don't you, M. Poirot?'

Poirot shook his head in a perplexed manner.

'This telegram complicates the affair,' he murmured. 'But we must be quick – extremely quick.'

Mr Satterthwaite did not see the need for extreme haste, but he agreed politely.

'Certainly, we will go by the first train in the morning. Er – that is to say, is it necessary for us all to go?'

'Sir Charles and I had arranged to go down to Gilling,' said Egg.

'We can postpone that,' said Sir Charles.

'I don't think we ought to postpone anything,' said Egg. 'There is no need for all four of us to go to Yorkshire. It's absurd. Mass formation. M. Poirot and Mr Satterthwaite go to Yorkshire and Sir Charles and I go to Gilling.'

'I'd rather like to look into this Rushbridger business,' said Sir Charles with a trace of wistfulness. 'You see, I – er – talked to the Matron before – got my foot in, so to speak.'

'That's just why you'd better keep away,' said Egg. 'You involved yourself in a lot of lies, and now this Rushbridger woman has come to herself you'll be exposed as a thorough-paced liar. It's far far more important that you should come to Gilling. If we want to see Miss Milray's mother she'll open out to you much more than she would to anyone else. You're her daughter's employer, and she'll have confidence in you.'

Sir Charles looked into Egg's glowing, earnest face.

'I'll come to Gilling,' he said. 'I think you're quite right.'

'I know I'm right,' said Egg.

'In my opinion an excellent arrangement,' said Poirot briskly. 'As mademoiselle says, Sir Charles is pre-eminently the person to interview this Mrs Milray. Who knows, you may learn from her facts of much more importance than those we shall learn in Yorkshire.'

Matters were arranged on this basis, and the following morning Sir Charles picked up Egg in his car at a quarter to ten. Poirot and Mr Satterthwaite had already left London by train.

It was a lovely crisp morning, with just a touch of frost in the air. Egg felt her spirits rising as they turned and twisted through the various short cuts which Sir Charles's experience had discovered south of the Thames.

At last, however, they were flying smoothly along the Folkestone road. After passing through Maidstone, Sir Charles consulted a map, and they turned off from the main road and were shortly winding through country lanes. It was about a quarter to twelve when they at last reached their objective.

Gilling was a village which the world had left behind. It had an old church, a vicarage, two or three shops, a row of cottages, three or four new council houses and a very attractive village green.

Miss Milray's mother lived in a tiny house on the other side of the green to the church.

As the car drew up Egg asked:

Agatha Christie

'Does Miss Milray know you are going to see her mother?'

'Oh, yes. She wrote to prepare the old lady.'

'Do you think that was a good thing?'

'My dear child, why not?'

'Oh, I don't know . . . You didn't bring her down with you, though.'

'As a matter of fact, I thought she might cramp my style. She's so much more efficient than I am – she'd probably try to prompt me.'

Egg laughed.

Mrs Milray turned out to be almost ludicrously unlike her daughter. Where Miss Milray was hard, she was soft, where Miss Milray was angular, she was round. Mrs Milray was an immense dumpling of a woman immovably fixed in an armchair conveniently placed so that she could, from the window, observe all that went on in the world outside.

She seemed pleasurably excited by the arrival of her visitors.

'This is very nice of you, I'm sure, Sir Charles. I've heard so much about you from my Violet.' (Violet! Singularly incongruous name for Miss Milray.) 'You don't know how much she admires you. It's been most interesting for her working with you all these years. Won't you sit down, Miss Lytton Gore? You'll excuse my not getting up. I've lost the use of my limbs for many years now. The Lord's will, and I don't complain, and what I say is one can get used to anything. Perhaps you'd like a little refreshment after your drive down?'

Both Sir Charles and Egg disclaimed the need of refreshment, but Mrs Milray paid no attention. She clapped her hands in an Oriental manner, and tea and biscuits made their appearance. As they nibbled and sipped, Sir Charles came to the object of their visit.

'I expect you've heard, Mrs Milray, all about the tragic death of Mr Babbington who used to be vicar here?'

The dumpling nodded its head in vigorous assent.

'Yes, indeed. I've read all about the exhumation in the paper. And whoever can have poisoned him I can't imagine. A very nice man, he was, everyone liked him here – and her, too. And their little children and all.'

'It is indeed a great mystery,' said Sir Charles. 'We're all in despair about it. In fact, we wondered if you could possibly throw any light upon the matter.'

'Me? But I haven't seen the Babbingtons – let me see – it must be over fifteen years.'

'I know, but some of us have the idea that there might be something in the past to account for his death.'

'I'm sure I don't know what there could be. They led very quiet lives – very badly off, poor things, with all those children.'

Agatha Christie

Mrs Milray was willing enough to reminisce, but her reminiscences seemed to shed little light on the problem they had set out to solve.

Sir Charles showed her the enlargement of a snapshot which included the Dacres, also an early portrait of Angela Sutcliffe and a somewhat blurred reproduction of Miss Wills cut from a newspaper. Mrs Milray surveyed them all with great interest, but with no signs of recognition.

'I can't say I remember any of them – of course it's a long time ago. But this is a small place. There's not much coming and going. The Agnew girls, the doctor's daughters – they're all married and out in the world, and our present doctor's a bachelor – he's got a new young partner. Then there were the old Miss Cayleys – sat in the big pew – they're all dead many years back. And the Richardsons – he died and she went to Wales. And the village people, of course. But there's not much change there. Violet, I expect, could tell you as much as I could. She was a young girl then and often over at the Vicarage.'

Sir Charles tried to envisage Miss Milray as a young girl and failed.

He asked Mrs Milray if she remembered anyone of the name of Rushbridger, but the name failed to evoke any response.

Finally they took their leave.

Their next move was a scratch lunch in the baker's shop. Sir Charles had hankerings for fleshpots elsewhere, but Egg pointed out that they might get hold of some local gossip.

'And boiled eggs and scones will do you no harm for once,' she said severely. 'Men are so fussy about their food.'

'I always find eggs so depressing,' said Sir Charles meekly.

The woman who served them was communicative enough. She, too, had read of the exhumation in the paper and had been proportionately thrilled by its being 'old vicar'. 'I were a child at the time,' she explained. 'But I remember him.'

She could not, however, tell them much about him.

After lunch they went to the church and looked through the register of births, marriages and deaths. Here again there seemed nothing hopeful or suggestive.

They came out into the churchyard and lingered. Egg read the names on the tombstones.

'What queer names there are,' she said. 'Listen, here's a whole family of Stavepennys and here's a Mary Ann Sticklepath.'

'None of them so queer as mine,' murmured Sir Charles.

'Cartwright? I don't think that's a queer name at all.'

'I didn't mean Cartwright. Cartwright's my acting name, and I finally adopted it legally.'

'What's your real name?'

'I couldn't possibly tell you. It's my guilty secret.'

'Is it as terrible as all that?'

'It's not so much terrible as humorous.'

'Oh – tell it me.'

'Certainly not,' said Sir Charles firmly.

'Please.'

'No.'

'Why not?'

'You'd laugh.'

'I wouldn't.'

'You wouldn't be able to help laughing.'

'Oh, please tell me. Please, please, please.'

'What a persistent creature you are, Egg. Why do you want to know?'

'Because you won't tell me.'

'You adorable child,' said Sir Charles a little unsteadily.

'I'm not a child.'

'Aren't you? I wonder.'

'Tell me,' whispered Egg softly.

A humorous and rueful smile twisted Sir Charles's mouth.

'Very well, here goes. My father's name was Mugg.'

'Not really?'

'Really and truly.'

'H'm,' said Egg. 'That is a bit catastrophic. To go through life as Mugg –'

'Wouldn't have taken me far in my career, I agree. I remember,' went on Sir Charles dreamily, 'I played with the idea (I was young then) of calling myself Ludovic Castiglione – but I eventually compromised on British alliteration as Charles Cartwright.'

'Are you really Charles?'

'Yes, my godfathers and godmothers saw to that.' He hesitated, then said, 'Why don't you say Charles – and drop the Sir?'

'I might.'

'You did yesterday. When – when – you thought I was dead.'

'Oh, then.' Egg tried to make her voice nonchalant.

Sir Charles said abruptly: 'Egg, somehow or other this murder business doesn't seem real any more. Today especially, it seems fantastic. I meant to clear the thing up before – before anything else. I've been superstitious about it. I've associated success in solving problems with – with another kind of success. Oh, damn, why do I beat about the bush? I've made love on the stage so often that I'm diffident about it in real life . . . Is it me or is it young Manders, Egg? I must know. Yesterday I thought it was me . . .'

'You thought right . . .'

'You incredible angel,' cried Sir Charles.

'Charles, Charles, you can't kiss me in a church-yard . . .'

'I shall kiss you anywhere I please . . .'

II

'We've found out nothing,' said Egg later, as they were speeding back to London.

'Nonsense, we've found out the only thing worth finding out . . . What do I care about dead clergymen or dead doctors? You're the only thing that matters . . . You know, my dear, I'm thirty years older than you – are you sure it doesn't matter?'

Egg pinched his arm gently.

'Don't be silly . . . I wonder if the others have found out anything?'

'They're welcome to it,' said Sir Charles generously.

'Charles – you used to be so keen.'

But Sir Charles was no longer playing the part of the great detective.

'Well, it was my own show. Now I've handed over to Moustachios. It's his business.'

'Do you think he really knows who committed the crimes? He said he did.'

'Probably hasn't the faintest idea, but he's got to keep up his professional reputation.'

Egg was silent. Sir Charles said:

'What are you thinking about, darling?'

'I was thinking about Miss Milray. She was so odd in her manner that evening I told you about. She had just bought the paper about the exhumation, and she said she didn't know what to do.'

'Nonsense,' said Sir Charles cheerfully. 'That woman always knows what to do.'

'Do be serious, Charles. She sounded – worried.'

'Egg, my sweet, what do I care for Miss Milray's worries? What do I care for anything but you and me?'

'You'd better pay some attention to the trams!' said Egg. 'I don't want to be widowed before I'm a wife.'

They arrived back at Sir Charles's flat for tea. Miss Milray came out to meet them.

'There is a telegram for you, Sir Charles.'

'Thank you, Miss Milray.' He laughed, a nervous boyish laugh. 'Look here, I must tell you our news. Miss Lytton Gore and I are going to get married.'

There was a moment's pause, and then Miss Milray said:

'Oh! I'm sure – I'm sure you'll be very happy.'

There was a queer note in her voice. Egg noticed it, but before she could formulate her impression Charles

Agatha Christie

Cartwright had swung round to her with a quick exclamation.

'My God, Egg, look at this. It's from Satterthwaite.'

He shoved the telegram into her hands. Egg read it, and her eyes opened wide.

Mrs De Rushbridger

Before catching their train Hercule Poirot and Mr Satterthwaite had had a brief interview with Miss Lyndon, the late Sir Bartholomew Strange's secretary. Miss Lyndon had been very willing to help, but had had nothing of importance to tell them. Mrs de Rushbridger was only mentioned in Sir Bartholomew's case book in a purely professional fashion. Sir Bartholomew had never spoken of her save in medical terms.

The two men arrived at the Sanatorium about twelve o'clock. The maid who opened the door looked excited and flushed. Mr Satterthwaite asked first for the Matron.

'I don't know whether she can see you this morning,' said the girl doubtfully.

Mr Satterthwaite extracted a card and wrote a few words on it.

'Please take her this.'

Agatha Christie

They were shown into a small waiting-room. In about five minutes the door opened and the Matron came in. She was looking quite unlike her usual brisk efficient self.

Mr Satterthwaite rose.

'I hope you remember me' he said. 'I came here with Sir Charles Cartwright just after the death of Sir Bartholomew Strange.'

'Yes, indeed, Mr Satterthwaite, of course I remember; and Sir Charles asked after poor Mrs de Rushbridger then, and it seems such a coincidence.'

'Let me introduce M. Hercule Poirot.'

Poirot bowed and the Matron responded absently. She went on:

'I can't understand how you can have had a telegram as you say. The whole thing seems most mysterious. Surely it can't be connected with the poor doctor's death in any way? There must be some madman about – that's the only way I can account for it. Having the police here and everything. It's really been terrible.'

'The police?' said Mr Satterthwaite, surprised.

'Yes, since ten o'clock they've been here.'

'The police?' said Hercule Poirot.

'Perhaps we could see Mrs de Rushbridger now,' suggested Mr Satterthwaite. 'Since she asked us to come –'

The Matron interrupted him.

'Oh, Mr Satterthwaite, then you don't know!'

'Know what?' demanded Poirot sharply.

'Poor Mrs de Rushbridger. She's dead.'

'Dead?' cried Poirot. '*Mille Tonnerres*! That explains it. Yes, that explains it. I should have seen—' He broke off. 'How did she die?'

'It's most mysterious. A box of chocolates came for her – liqueur chocolates – by post. She ate one – it must have tasted horrible, but she was taken by surprise, I suppose, and she swallowed it. One doesn't like spitting a thing out.'

'*Oui, oui*, and if a liquid runs suddenly down your throat, it is difficult.'

'So she swallowed it and called out and Nurse came rushing, but we couldn't do anything. She died in about two minutes. Then doctor sent for the police, and they came and examined the chocolates. All the top layer had been tampered with, the underneath ones were all right.'

'And the poison employed?'

'They think it's nicotine.'

'Yes,' said Poirot. 'Again nicotine. What a stroke! What an audacious stroke!'

'We are too late,' said Mr Satterthwaite. 'We shall never know now what she had to tell us. Unless – unless – she confided in someone?' He glanced interrogatively at the Matron.

Poirot shook his head.

'There will have been no confidences, you will find.'

'We can ask,' said Mr Satterthwaite. 'One of the nurses, perhaps?'

'By all means ask,' said Poirot; but he did not sound hopeful.

Mr Satterthwaite turned to the Matron who immediately sent for the two nurses, on day and night duty respectively, who had been in attendance on Mrs de Rushbridger, but neither of them could add any information to that already given. Mrs de Rushbridger had never mentioned Sir Bartholomew's death, and they did not even know of the despatching of the telegram.

On a request from Poirot, the two men were taken to the dead woman's room. They found Superintendent Crossfield in charge, and Mr Satterthwaite introduced him to Poirot.

Then the two men moved over to the bed and stood looking down on the dead woman. She was about forty, dark-haired and pale. Her face was not peaceful – it still showed the agony of her death.

Mr Satterthwaite said slowly:

'Poor soul . . .'

He looked across at Hercule Poirot. There was a strange expression on the little Belgian's face. Something about it made Mr Satterthwaite shiver . . .

Mr Satterthwaite said:

'Someone knew she was going to speak, and killed her . . . She was killed in order to prevent her speaking . . .'

Poirot nodded.

'Yes, that is so.'

'She was murdered to prevent her telling us what she knew.'

'Or what she did not know . . . But let us not waste time . . . There is much to be done. *There must be no more deaths.* We must see to that.'

Mr Satterthwaite asked curiously:

'Does this fit in with your idea of the murderer's identity?'

'Yes, it fits . . . But I realize one thing: The murderer is more dangerous than I thought . . . We must be careful.'

Superintendent Crossfield followed them out of the room and learnt from them of the telegram which had been received by them. The telegram had been handed in at Melfort Post Office, and on inquiry there it was elicited that it had been handed in by a small boy. The young lady in charge remembered it, because the message had excited her very much, mentioning, as it did, Sir Bartholomew Strange's death.

After some lunch in company with the superintendent, and after despatching a telegram to Sir Charles, the quest was resumed.

Agatha Christie

At six o'clock that evening the small boy who had handed in the telegram was found. He told his story promptly. He had been given the telegram by a man dressed in shabby clothes. The man told him that the telegram had been given him by a 'loony lady' in the 'House in the Park'. She had dropped it out of the window wrapped round two half-crowns. The man was afraid to be mixed up in some funny business, and was tramping in the other direction, so he had given the boy two and six and told him to keep the change.

A search would be instituted for the man. In the meantime there seemed nothing more to be done, and Poirot and Mr Satterthwaite returned to London.

It was close on midnight when the two men arrived back in town. Egg had gone back to her mother, but Sir Charles met them, and the three men discussed the situation.

'*Mon ami*,' said Poirot, 'be guided by me. Only one thing will solve this case – the little grey cells of the brain. To rush up and down England, to hope that this person and that will tell us what we want to know – all such methods are amateurish and absurd. The truth can only be seen from within.'

Sir Charles looked slightly sceptical.

'What do you want to do, then?'

'I want to think. I ask of you twenty-four hours – in which to think.'

Sir Charles shook his head with a slight smile.

'Will thinking tell you what it was this woman could have said if she lived?'

'I believe so.'

'It hardly seems possible. However, M. Poirot, you must have it your own way. If you can see through this mystery, it's more than I can. I'm beaten, and I confess it. In any case, I've other fish to fry.'

Perhaps he hoped to be questioned, but if so his expectation was disappointed. Mr Satterthwaite did indeed look up alertly, but Poirot remained lost in thought.

'Well, I must be off,' said the actor. 'Oh, just one thing. I'm rather worried about – Miss Wills.'

'What about her?'

'She's gone.'

Poirot stared at him.

'Gone? Gone where?'

'Nobody knows . . . I was thinking things over after I got your telegram. As I told you at the time, I felt convinced that that woman knew something she hadn't told us. I thought I'd have a last shot at getting it out of her. I drove out to her house – it was about half-past nine when I got there – and asked for her. It appears she left home this morning – went up to London for the day – that's what she said. Her people got a telegram in the evening saying she wasn't returning for a day or so and not to worry.'

'And were they worrying?'

'I gather they were, rather. You see, she hadn't taken any luggage with her.'

'Odd,' murmured Poirot.

'I know. It seems as though – I don't know. I feel uneasy.'

'I warned her,' said Poirot. 'I warned everyone. You remember I said to them, "Speak now."'

'Yes, yes. Do you think that she, too –?'

'I have my ideas,' said Poirot. 'For the moment I prefer not to discuss them.'

'First, the butler – Ellis – then Miss Wills. Where is Ellis? It's incredible that the police have never been able to lay hands on him.'

'They have not looked for his body in the right place,' said Poirot.

'Then you agree with Egg. You think he is dead?'

'Ellis will never be seen alive again.'

'My God,' burst out Sir Charles. 'It's a nightmare – the whole thing is utterly incomprehensible.'

'No, no. It is sane and logical, on the contrary.'

Sir Charles stared at him.

'You say that?'

'Certainly. You see, I have the orderly mind.'

'I don't understand you.'

Mr Satterthwaite, too, looked curiously at the little detective.

'What kind of a mind have I?' demanded Sir Charles, slightly hurt.

'You have the actor's mind, Sir Charles, creative, original, seeing always dramatic values. Mr Satterthwaite here, he has the playgoer's mind, he observes the characters, he has the sense of atmosphere. But me, I have the prosaic mind. I see only the facts without any dramatic trappings or footlights.'

'Then we're to leave you to it?'

'That is my idea. For twenty-four hours.'

'Good luck to you, then. Goodnight.'

As they went away together Sir Charles said to Mr Satterthwaite:

'That chap thinks a lot of himself.'

He spoke rather coldly.

Mr Satterthwaite smiled. The star part! So that was it. He said:

'What did you mean by saying you had other fish to fry, Sir Charles?'

On Sir Charles's face appeared the sheepish expression that Mr Satterthwaite knew so well from attending weddings in Hanover Square.

'Well, as a matter of fact, I – er – well, Egg and I –'

'I'm delighted to hear it,' said Mr Satterthwaite. 'My best congratulations.'

'Of course I'm years too old for her.'

'She doesn't think so – and she's the best judge.'

'That's very nice of you, Satterthwaite. You know, I'd got it into my head she was fond of young Manders.'

'I wonder what made you think that,' said Mr Satterthwaite innocently.

'Anyway,' said Sir Charles firmly, 'she isn't . . .'

286

Chapter 14
Miss Milray

Poirot did not have quite the uninterrupted twenty-four hours for which he had stipulated.

At twenty minutes past eleven on the following morning Egg walked in unannounced. To her amazement she found the great detective engaged in building card houses. Her face showed such lively scorn that Poirot was impelled to defend himself.

'It is not, mademoiselle, that I have become childish in my old age. No. But the building of card houses, I have always found it most stimulating to the mind. It is an old habit of mine. This morning, first thing, I go out and buy the pack of cards. Unfortunately I make an error, they are not real cards. But they do just as well.'

Egg looked more closely at the erection on the table.

She laughed.

'Good heavens, they've sold you Happy Families.'

'What is that you say, the Happy Family?'

'Yes, it's a game. Children play it in the nursery.'

'Ah, well, one can compose the houses just in the same manner.'

Egg had picked up some of the cards from the table and was looking at them affectionately.

'Master Bun, the baker's son – I always loved him. And here's Mrs Mug, the milkman's wife. Oh, dear, I suppose that's me.'

'Why is that funny picture you, mademoiselle?'

'Because of the name.'

Egg laughed at his bewildered face and then began explaining. When she had finished he said:

'Ah, it was that that Sir Charles meant last night. I wondered . . . Mugg – ah, yes, one says in slang, does one not, you are a *mug* – a fool? Naturally you would change your name. You would not like to be the Lady Mugg, eh?'

Egg laughed. She said:

'Well, wish me happiness.'

'I do wish you happiness, mademoiselle. Not the brief happiness of youth, but the happiness that endures – the happiness that is built upon a rock.'

'I'll tell Charles you call him a rock,' said Egg. 'And now for what I came to see you about. I've been worrying and worrying about that cutting from the paper that Oliver dropped from his wallet. You know, the one Miss Wills picked up and handed back to him. It seems to me that either Oliver is telling a downright lie when he says he doesn't remember its being there, *or else it never was there.* He dropped some odd bit of paper, and that woman pretended it was the nicotine cutting.'

'Why should she have done that, mademoiselle?'

'Because she wanted to get rid of it. She planted it on Oliver.'

'You mean she is the criminal?'

'Yes.'

'What was her motive?'

'It's no good asking me that. I can only suggest that she's a lunatic. Clever people often are rather mad. I can't see any other reason – in fact I can't see any motive anywhere.'

'Decidedly, that is the *impasse.* I should not ask *you* to guess at a motive. It is of myself that I ask that question without ceasing. *What was the motive behind Mr Babbington's death*? When I can answer that the case will be solved.'

'You don't think just madness –?' suggested Egg.

'No, mademoiselle – not madness in the sense you mean. There is a *reason.* I must find that reason.'

'Well, goodbye,' said Egg. 'I'm sorry to have disturbed you, but the idea just occurred to me. I must hurry. I'm going with Charles to the dress rehearsal of *Little Dog Laughed* – you know, the play Miss Wills has written for Angela Sutcliffe. It's the first night tomorrow.'

'*Mon dieu!*' cried Poirot.

'What is it? Has anything happened?'

'Yes, indeed something has happened. An idea. A superb idea. Oh, but I have been blind – blind –'

Egg stared at him. As though realizing his eccentricity, Poirot took a hold on himself. He patted Egg on the shoulder.

'You think I am mad. Not at all. I heard what you said. You go to see '*The Little Dog Laughed*, and Miss Sutcliffe acts in it. Go then, and pay no attention to what I have said.'

Rather doubtfully Egg departed. Left to himself, Poirot strode up and down the room muttering under his breath. His eyes shone green as any cat's.

'*Mais oui* – that explains everything. A curious motive – a very curious motive – such a motive as I have never come across before, and yet it is reasonable, and, given the circumstances, natural. Altogether a very curious case.'

He passed the table where his card house still reposed. With a sweep of his hands he swept the cards from the table.

'The happy family, I need it no longer,' he said. 'The problem is solved. It only remains to act.'

He caught up his hat and put on his overcoat. Then he went downstairs and the commissionaire called him a taxi. Poirot gave the address of Sir Charles's flat.

Arrived there, he paid off the taxi, and stepped into the hall. The porter was absent taking up the lift. Poirot walked up the stairs. Just as he arrived on the second floor the door of Sir Charles's flat opened and Miss Milray came out.

She started when she saw Poirot.

'You!'

Poirot smiled.

'Me! Or is it I? *Enfin, moi!*'

Miss Milray said:

'I'm afraid you won't find Sir Charles. He's gone to the Babylon Theatre with Miss Lytton Gore.'

'It is not Sir Charles I seek. It is my stick that I think I have left behind one day.'

'Oh, I see. Well, if you'll ring, Temple will find it for you. I'm sorry I can't stop. I'm on my way to catch a train. I'm going down to Kent – to my mother.'

'I comprehend. Do not let me delay you, mademoiselle.'

He stood aside and Miss Milray passed rapidly down the stairs. She was carrying a small attaché case.

But when she had gone Poirot seemed to forget the purpose for which he had come. Instead of going on up to the landing, he turned and made his way downstairs again. He arrived at the front door just in time to see Miss Milray getting into a taxi. Another taxi was coming slowly along the kerb. Poirot raised a hand and it came to rest. He got in and directed the driver to follow the other taxi.

No surprise showed on his face when the first taxi went north and finally drew up at Paddington Station, though Paddington is an odd station from which to proceed to Kent. Poirot went to the first-class booking window and demanded a return ticket to Loomouth. The train was due to depart in five minutes. Pulling up his overcoat well about his ears, for the day was cold, Poirot ensconced himself in the corner of a first-class carriage.

They arrived at Loomouth about five o'clock. It was already growing dark. Standing back a little, Poirot heard Miss Milray being greeted by the friendly porter at the little station.

'Well, now, miss, we didn't expect you. Is Sir Charles coming down?'

Miss Milray replied:

'I've come down here unexpectedly. I shall be going back tomorrow morning. I've just come to fetch some things. No, I don't want a cab, thank you. I'll walk up by the cliff path.'

The dusk had deepened. Miss Milray walked briskly up the steep zigzag path. A good way behind came

Hercule Poirot. He trod softly like a cat. Miss Milray, on arrival at Crow's Nest, produced a key from her bag and passed through the side door, leaving it ajar. She reappeared a minute or two later. She had a rusty door key and an electric torch in her hand. Poirot drew back a little behind a convenient bush.

Miss Milray passed round behind the house and up a scrambling overgrown path. Hercule Poirot followed. Up and up went Miss Milray until she came suddenly to an old stone tower such as is found often on that coast. This one was of humble and dilapidated appearance. There was, however, a curtain over the dirty window, and Miss Milray inserted her key in the big wooden door.

The key turned with a protesting creak. The door swung with a groan on its hinges. Miss Milray and her torch passed inside.

With an increase of pace Poirot caught up. He passed, in his turn, noiselessly through the door. The light of Miss Milray's torch gleamed fitfully on glass retorts, a bunsen burner – various apparatus.

Miss Milray had picked up a crowbar. She had raised it and was holding it over the glass apparatus when a hand caught her by the arm. She gasped and turned.

The green, catlike eyes of Poirot looked into hers.

'You cannot do that, mademoiselle,' he said. 'For what you seek to destroy is evidence.'

Curtain

Hercule Poirot sat in a big arm-chair. The wall lights had been turned out. Only a rose-shaded lamp shed its glow on the figure in the arm-chair. There seemed something symbolic about it – he alone in the light – and the other three, Sir Charles, Mr Satterthwaite and Egg Lytton Gore – Poirot's audience – sitting in the outer darkness.

Hercule Poirot's voice was dreamy. He seemed to be addressing himself to space rather than to his listeners.

'To reconstruct the crime – that is the aim of the detective. To reconstruct a crime you must place one fact upon another just as you place one card on another in building a house of cards. And if the facts will not fit – if the card will not balance – well – you must start your house again, or else it will fall . . .

'As I said the other day, there are three different

types of mind: There is the dramatic mind – the producer's mind, which sees the effect of reality that can be produced by mechanical appliances – there is also the mind that reacts easily to dramatic appearances – and there is the young romantic mind – and finally, my friends, there is the prosaic mind – the mind that sees not blue sea and mimosa trees, but the painted backcloth of stage scenery.

'So I come, *mes amis*, to the murder of Stephen Babbington in August last. On that evening Sir Charles Cartwright advanced the theory that Stephen Babbington had been murdered. I did not agree with that theory. I could not believe (a) that such a man as Stephen Babbington was likely to have been murdered, and (b) that it was possible to administer poison to a particular person under the circumstances that had obtained that evening.

'Now here I admit that Sir Charles was right and I was wrong. I was wrong because I was looking at the crime from an entirely false angle. It is only twenty-four hours ago that I suddenly perceived the proper angle of vision – and let me say that from that angle of vision the murder of Stephen Babbington is both *reasonable* and *possible*.

'But I will pass from that point for the moment and take you step by step along the path I myself have trodden. The death of Stephen Babbington I may call the first act of our drama. The curtain fell on that act when we all departed from Crow's Nest.

'What I might call the second act of the drama began in Monte Carlo when Mr Satterthwaite showed me the newspaper account of Sir Bartholomew's death. It was at once clear that I had been wrong and Sir Charles had been right. Both Stephen Babbington and Sir Bartholomew Strange had been murdered and the two murders formed part of one and the same crime. Later a third murder completed the series – the murder of Mrs de Rushbridger. What we need, therefore, is a reasonable common-sense theory which will link those three deaths together – in other words those three crimes were committed by one and the same person, and were to the advantage and benefit of that particular person.

'Now I may say at once that the principal thing that worried me was the fact that the murder of Sir Bartholomew Strange came *after* that of Stephen Babbington. Looking at those three murders without distinction of time and place the probabilities pointed to the murder of Sir Bartholomew Strange being what one might call the central or principal crime, and the other two murders as secondary in character – that is, arising from the connection of those two people with Sir Bartholomew Strange. However, as I remarked before – one cannot have one's crime as one would like to have it. Stephen Babbington had been murdered first and Sir Bartholomew Strange some time later. It seemed, therefore, as though the second crime must necessarily arise out of the first and that accordingly it was the first crime we must examine for the clue to the whole.

'I did indeed so far incline to the theory of probability that I seriously considered the idea of a *mistake* having arisen. Was it possible that Sir Bartholomew Strange was intended as the first victim, and that Mr Babbington was poisoned by mistake? I was forced, however, to abandon that idea. Anybody who knew Sir Bartholomew Strange with any degree of intimacy knew that he disliked the cocktail habit.

'Another suggestion: Had Stephen Babbington been poisoned in mistake for any other member of the original party? I could not find any evidence of such a thing. I was therefore forced back to the conclusion that the murder of Stephen Babbington had been definitely *intended* – and at once I came up against a complete stumbling block – the apparent *impossibility* of such a thing having happened.

'One should always start an investigation with the simplest and most obvious theories. Granting that Stephen Babbington had drunk a poisoned cocktail, who had had the opportunity of poisoning that cocktail? At first sight, it seemed to me that the only two people who could have done so (e.g., who handled the drinks) were Sir Charles Cartwright himself and the parlourmaid Temple. But though either of them could presumably have introduced the poison into the glass, *neither of them had had any opportunity of directing that particular glass into Mr Babbington's hand.* Temple might have done so by adroit handing of the tray so as to offer him the one remaining glass – (not easy, but it might have been done). Sir Charles could have done so by deliberately picking up the particular glass and handing it to him. But neither of these things had occurred. It looked as though *chance* and *chance* alone directed that particular glass to Stephen Babbington.

'Sir Charles Cartwright and Temple had the handling of the cocktails. Were either of those two at Melfort Abbey? They were not. Who had the best chance of tampering with Sir Bartholomew's port glass? The absconding butler, Ellis, and his helper, the parlourmaid. But here, however, the possibility that one of the guests had done so could not be laid aside. It was risky, but it was possible, for any of the house-party to have slipped into the dining-room and put the nicotine into the port glass.

'When I joined you at Crow's Nest you already had a list drawn up of the people who had been at Crow's Nest and at Melfort Abbey. I may say now that the four names which headed the list – Captain and Mrs

Agatha Christie

Dacres, Miss Sutcliffe and Miss Wills – I discarded immediately.

'It was *impossible* that any of those four people should have known *beforehand* that they were going to meet Stephen Babbington at dinner. The employment of nicotine as a poison showed a carefully thought-out plan, not one that could be put into operation on the spur of the moment. There were three other names on that list – Lady Mary Lytton Gore, Miss Lytton Gore and Mr Oliver Manders. Although not probable, those three were *possible*. They were local people, they might conceivably have motives for the removal of Stephen Babbington, and have chosen the evening of the dinner-party for putting their plans into operation.

'On the other hand, I could find no evidence whatsoever that any of them had actually done such a thing.

'Mr Satterthwaite, I think, reasoned on much the same lines as I had done, and he fixed his suspicions on Oliver Manders. I may say that young Manders was by far the most possible suspect. He displayed all the signs of high nervous tension on that evening at Crow's Nest – he had a somewhat distorted view of life owing to his private troubles – he had a strong inferiority complex, which is a frequent cause of crime, he was at an unbalanced age, he had actually had a quarrel, or shall we say had displayed animosity against Mr Babbington. Then there were the curious circumstances of his arrival at Melfort Abbey. And later we had his somewhat incredible story of the letter from Sir Bartholomew Strange and the evidence of Miss Wills as to his having a newspaper cutting on the subject of nicotine poisoning in his possession.

'Oliver Manders, then, was clearly the person who should be placed at the head of the list of those seven suspects.

'But then, my friends, I was visited by a curious sensation. It seemed clear and logical enough that the person who had committed the crimes *must have been a person who had been present on both occasions*; in other words *a person on that list of seven – but I had the feeling that that obviousness was an arranged obviousness*. It was what any sane and logical person would be *expected* to think. I felt that I was, in fact, looking not at reality but at an artfully painted bit of scenery. A really clever criminal would have realized that *anyone whose name was on that list would necessarily be suspect*, and therefore he or she would arrange for it not to be there.

'In other words, the murderer of Stephen Babbington and Sir Bartholomew Strange *was* present on both occasions – but was not *apparently* so.

'Who had been present on the first occasion and not on the second? Sir Charles Cartwright, Mr Satterthwaite, Miss Milray and Mr Babbington.

'Could any of those four have been present on the second occasion in some capacity other than their own? Sir Charles and Mr Satterthwaite had been in the South of France, Miss Milray had been in London, Mrs Babbington had been in Loomouth. Of the four, then, Miss Milray and Mrs Babbington seemed indicated. But could Miss Milray have been present at Melfort Abbey unrecognized by any of the company? Miss Milray has very striking features not easily disguised and not easily forgotten. I decided that it was impossible that Miss Milray could have been at Melfort Abbey unrecognized. The same applied to Mrs Babbington.

'For the matter of that could Mr Satterthwaite or Sir Charles Cartwright have been at Melfort Abbey and not been recognized? Mr Satterthwaite just possibly; but when we come to Sir Charles Cartwright we come to a very different matter. Sir Charles is an actor accustomed to playing a part. But what part could he have played?

'And then I came to the consideration of the butler Ellis.

'A very mysterious person, Ellis. A person who appears from nowhere a fortnight before the crime and vanishes afterwards with complete success. Why was Ellis so successful? *Because Ellis did not really exist.* Ellis, again, was a thing of pasteboard and paint and stagecraft – Ellis was not *real*.

'But was it *possible*? After all, the servants at Melfort Abbey knew Sir Charles Cartwright, and Sir Bartholomew Strange was an intimate friend of his. The servants I got over easily enough. The impersonation of the butler risked nothing – if the servants recognized him – why, no harm would be done – the whole thing could be passed off as a joke. If, on the other hand, a fortnight passed without any suspicion being aroused, well, the thing was safe as houses. And I recalled what I had been told of the servants' remarks about the butler. He was "quite the gentleman", and had been "in good houses", and knew several interesting scandals. That was easy enough. But a very significant statement was made by the parlourmaid Alice. She said, "He arranged the work different from any butler I ever knew before." When that remark was repeated to me, it became a confirmation of my theory.

'But Sir Bartholomew Strange was another matter. It is hardly to be supposed that his friend could take him in. He must have known of the impersonation. Had we any evidence of that? Yes. The acute Mr Satterthwaite pounced on one point quite early in the proceedings – the facetious remark of Sir Bartholomew (totally uncharacteristic of his manner to servants) – "You're a first-class butler, aren't you, Ellis?" *A perfectly understandable remark if the butler were Sir*

Agatha Christie

*Charles Cartwright and Sir Bartholomew was in on
the joke.*

'Because that is undoubtedly how Sir Bartholomew
saw the matter. The impersonation of Ellis was a joke,
possibly even a wager, its culmination was designed
to be the successful spoofing of the house-party –
hence Sir Bartholomew's remark about a surprise and
his cheerful humour. Note, too, that there was still
time to draw back. If any of the house-party had
spotted Charles Cartwright that first evening at the
dinner-table, nothing irrevocable had yet occurred.
The whole thing could have been passed off as a
joke. But nobody noticed the stooping middle-aged
butler, with his belladonna darkened eyes, and his
whiskers, and the painted birthmark on his wrist. A
very subtle identifying touch that – which completely
failed, owing to the lack of observation of most human
beings! The birthmark was intended to bulk largely in
the description of Ellis – and in all that fortnight no one
noticed it! The only person who did was the sharp-eyed
Miss Wills, to whom we shall come presently.

'What happened next? Sir Bartholomew died. This
time the death was not put down to natural causes.
The police came. They questioned Ellis and the others.
Later that night "Ellis" left by the secret passage,
resumed his own personality, and two days later was
strolling about the gardens at Monte Carlo ready to

be shocked and surprised by the news of his friend's death.

'This, mind you, was all theory. I had no actual proof, but everything that arose supported that theory. My house of cards was well and truly built. The blackmailing letters discovered in Ellis's room? But it was Sir Charles himself who discovered them!

'And what of the supposed letter from Sir Bartholomew Strange asking young Manders to arrange an accident? Well, what could be easier than for Sir Charles to write that letter in Sir Bartholomew's name? If Manders had not destroyed that letter himself, Sir Charles in the rôle of Ellis can easily do so when he valets the young gentleman. In the same way the newspaper cutting is easily introduced by Ellis into Oliver Manders's wallet.

'And now we come to the third victim – Mrs de Rushbridger. When do we first hear of Mrs de Rushbridger? Immediately after that very awkward chaffing reference to Ellis being the perfect butler – that extremely uncharacteristic utterance of Sir Bartholomew Strange. At all costs attention must be drawn away from Sir Bartholomew's manner to his butler. Sir Charles quickly asks what was the message the butler had brought. It is about this woman – this patient of the doctor's. And immediately Sir Charles throws all his personality into directing attention to this unknown woman and away from the butler. He goes to the Sanatorium and questions the Matron. He runs Mrs de Rushbridger for all he is worth as a red herring.

'We must now examine the part played by Miss Wills in the drama. Miss Wills has a curious personality. She is one of those people who are quite unable to impress themselves on their surroundings. She is neither good-looking nor witty nor clever, not even particularly sympathetic. She is nondescript. But she is extremely observant and extremely intelligent. She takes her revenge on the world with her pen. She has the great art of being able to reproduce character on paper. I do not know if there was anything about the butler that struck Miss Wills as unusual, but I do think that she was the only person at the table who noticed him at all. On the morning after the murder her insatiable curiosity led her to poke and pry, as the housemaid put it. She went into Dacres's room, she went through the baize door into the servants' quarters, led, I think, by the mongoose instinct for finding out.

'She was the only person who occasioned Sir Charles any uneasiness. That is why he was anxious to be the one to tackle her. He was fairly reassured by his interview and distinctly gratified that she had noticed the birthmark. But after that came catastrophe. I don't think that until that minute Miss Wills had connected Ellis the butler with Sir Charles Cartwright. I think she had only been vaguely struck by some resemblance to someone in Ellis. But she was an observer. When dishes were handed to her she had automatically noted – not the face – but the hands that held the dishes.

'It did not occur to her that *Ellis was Sir Charles*. But when Sir Charles was talking to her it did suddenly occur to her that *Sir Charles was Ellis*! And so she asked him to pretend to hand her a dish of vegetables. But it was not whether the birthmark was on the right or left wrist that interested her. She wanted a pretext to study his *hands* – hands held in the same position as those of Ellis the butler.

'And so she leaped to the truth. But she was a peculiar woman. She enjoyed knowledge for its own sake. Besides, she was by no means sure that Sir Charles had murdered his friend. He had masqueraded as a butler, yes – but that did not necessarily make him a murderer. Many an innocent man has kept silence because speech would place him in an awkward position.

'So Miss Wills kept her knowledge to herself – and enjoyed it. But Sir Charles was worried. He did not like that expression of satisfied malice on her face that he saw as he left the room. She knew something. What? Did it affect him? He could not be sure. But he felt that it was something connected with Ellis the butler. First Mr Satterthwaite – now Miss Wills. Attention *must* be drawn away from that vital point. It *must* be focused definitely elsewhere. And he thought of a plan – simple, audacious and, as he fancied, definitely mystifying.

'On the day of my Sherry Party I imagine Sir Charles rose very early, went to Yorkshire and, disguised in shabby clothes, gave the telegram to a small boy to send off. Then he returned to town in time to act the party I had indicated in my little drama. He did one more thing. *He posted a box of chocolates to a woman he had never seen and of whom he knew nothing . . .*

'You know what happened that evening. From Sir Charles's uneasiness I was fairly sure that Miss Wills had certain suspicions. When Sir Charles did his "death scene" I watched Miss Wills's face. I saw the look of astonishment that showed on it. I knew then that *Miss Wills definitely suspected Sir Charles of being the murderer.* When he appeared to die poisoned like the other two she thought her deductions must be wrong.

'But if Miss Wills suspected Sir Charles, then Miss Wills was in serious danger. A man who has killed twice will kill again. I uttered a very solemn warning. Later that night I communicated with Miss Wills by telephone, and on my advice she left home suddenly the next day. Since then she has been living here in this hotel. That I was wise is proved by the fact that Sir Charles went out to Tooting on the following evening after he had returned from Gilling. He was too late. The bird had flown.

'In the meantime, from his point of view, the plan had worked well. Mrs de Rushbridger had something of importance to tell us. Mrs de Rushbridger was killed before she could speak. How dramatic! How like the detective stories, the plays, the films! Again the cardboard and the tinsel and the painted cloth.

'But I, Hercule Poirot, was not deceived. Mr Satterthwaite said to me she was killed in order that she should not speak. I agreed. He went on to say she was killed before she could tell us what she knew. I said, "*Or what she did* NOT *know*." I think he was puzzled. But he should have seen then the truth. Mrs de Rushbridger was killed because she could, in actual fact, have told us *nothing at all*. Because she had no connection with the crime. If she were to be Sir Charles's successful red herring – she could only be so *dead*. And so Mrs de Rushbridger, a harmless stranger, was murdered . . .

'Yet even in that seeming triumph Sir Charles made a colossal – a childish – error! The telegram was addressed to me, Hercule Poirot, at the Ritz Hotel. But Mrs de Rushbridger had never heard of my connection with the case! No one up in that part of the world knew of it. It was an unbelievably childish error.

'*Eh bien*, then I had reached a certain stage. I knew the identity of the murderer. But I did not know the motive for the original crime.

'I reflected.

'And once again, more clearly than ever, I saw the death of Sir Bartholomew Strange as the original and purposeful murder. What reason could Sir Charles Cartwright have for the murder of his friend? Could I imagine a motive? I thought I could.'

There was a deep sigh. Sir Charles Cartwright rose slowly to his feet and strolled to the fireplace. He stood there, his hand on his hip, looking down at Poirot. His attitude (Mr Satterthwaite could have told you) was that of Lord Eaglemount as he looks scornfully at the rascally solicitor who has succeeded in fastening an accusation of fraud upon him. He radiated nobility and disgust. He was the aristocrat looking down at the ignoble canaille.

'You have an extraordinary imagination, M. Poirot,' he said. 'It's hardly worth while saying that there's not one single word of truth in your story. How you have the damned impertinence to dish up such an absurd fandangle of lies I don't know. But go on, I am interested. What was my motive for murdering a man whom I had known ever since boyhood?'

Hercule Poirot, the little bourgeois, looked up at the aristocrat. He spoke quickly but firmly.

'Sir Charles, we have a proverb that says, "*Cherchez la femme*." It was *there* that I found my motive. I had seen you with Mademoiselle Lytton Gore. It was clear that you loved her – loved her with that terrible absorbing passion that comes to a middle-aged man and which is usually inspired by an innocent young girl.

'You loved her. She, I could see, had the hero worship for you. You had only to speak and she would fall into your arms. But you did not speak. Why?

'You pretended to your friend, Mr Satterthwaite, that you were the dense lover who cannot recognize his mistress's answering passion. You pretended to think that Miss Lytton Gore was in love with Oliver Manders. But I say, Sir Charles, that you are a man of the world. You are a man with a great experience of women. *You cannot have been deceived.* You knew perfectly well that Miss Lytton Gore cared for you. Why, then, did you not marry her? You wanted to do so.

'It must be that there was some obstacle. What could that obstacle be? It could only be the fact that you already had a wife. But nobody ever spoke of you as a married man. You passed always as a bachelor. The marriage, then, had taken place when you were very young – before you became known as a rising young actor.

'What had happened to your wife? If she were

still alive, why did nobody know about her? If you were living apart there was the remedy of divorce. If your wife was a Catholic, or one who disapproved of divorce, she would still be known as living apart from you.

'But there are two tragedies where the law gives no relief. The woman you married might be serving a life sentence in some prison, or she might be confined in a lunatic asylum. *In neither case could you obtain a divorce*, and if it had happened while you were still a boy nobody might know about it.

'If nobody knew, you might marry Miss Lytton Gore without telling her the truth. *But supposing one person knew* – a friend who had known you all your life? Sir Bartholomew Strange was an honourabe, upright physician. He might pity you deeply, he might sympathize with a liaison or an irregular life, but he would not stand by silent and see you enter into a bigamous marriage with an unsuspecting young girl.

'Before you could marry Miss Lytton Gore, Sir Bartholomew Strange must be removed . . .'

Sir Charles laughed.

'And dear old Babbington? Did he know all about it, too?'

'I fancied so at first. But I soon found that there was no evidence to support that theory. Besides, my original stumbling block remained. *Even if it was you*

*who put the nicotine into the cocktail glass, you could not
have ensured its reaching one particular person.*

'That was my problem. And suddenly a chance word
from Miss Lytton Gore showed me light.

'The poison was not intended especially for Stephen
Babbington. It was intended for *any one* of those present,
with three exceptions. These exceptions were Miss
Lytton Gore, to whom you were careful to hand an
innocent glass, yourself, and Sir Bartholomew Strange,
who, you knew, did not drink cocktails.'

Mr Satterthwaite cried out:

'But that's nonsense! What's the point of it? There
isn't any.'

Poirot turned towards him. Triumph came into his
voice.

'Oh, yes, there is. A queer point – a very queer
point. The only time I have come across such a motive
for murder. The murder of Stephen Babbington was
neither more nor less than a *dress rehearsal.*'

'*What?*'

'Yes, Sir Charles was an actor. He obeyed his actor's
instinct. He tried out his murder before committing it.
No suspicion could possibly attach to him. Not one of
those people's deaths could benefit him in any way,
and, moreover, as everyone has found, *he could not
have been proved to have poisoned any particular person.*
And, my friends, the dress rehearsal went well. Mr

Agatha Christie

Babbington dies, and foul play is not even suspected. It is left to Sir Charles to urge that suspicion and he is highly gratified at our refusal to take it seriously. The substitution of the glass, too, that has gone without a hitch. In fact, he can be sure that, when the real performance comes, it will be "all right on the night".

'As you know, events took a slightly different turn. On the second occasion a doctor was present who immediately suspected poison. It was then to Sir Charles's interests to stress the death of Babbington. Sir Bartholomew's death must be presumed to be the outcome of the earlier death. Attention must be focused on the motive for Babbington's murder, not on any motive that might exist for Sir Bartholomew's removal.

'But there was one thing that Sir Charles failed to realize – the efficient watchfulness of Miss Milray. Miss Milray knew that her employer dabbled in chemical experiments in the tower in the garden. Miss Milray paid bills for rose spraying solution, and realized that quite a lot of it had unaccountably disappeared. When she read that Mr Babbington had died of nicotine poisoning, her clever brain leaped at once to the conclusion that Sir Charles had extracted the pure alkaloid from the rose solution.

'And Miss Milray did not know what to do, for she had known Mr Babbington as a little girl, and she was in love, deeply and devotedly as an ugly woman can be, with her fascinating employer.

'In the end she decided to destroy Sir Charles's apparatus. Sir Charles himself had been so cocksure of his success that he had never thought it necessary. She went down to Cornwall, and I followed.'

Again Sir Charles laughed. More than ever he looked a fine gentleman disgusted by a rat.

'Is some old chemical apparatus all your evidence?' he demanded contemptuously.

'No,' said Poirot. 'There is your passport showing the dates when you returned to and left England. And there is the fact that in the Harverton County Asylum there is a woman, Gladys Mary Mugg, the wife of Charles Mugg.'

Egg had so far sat silent – a frozen figure. But now she stirred. A little cry – almost a moan – came from her.

Sir Charles turned superbly.

'Egg, you don't believe a word of this absurd story, do you?'

He laughed. His hands were outstretched.

Egg came slowly forward as though hypnotized. Her eyes, appealing, tortured, gazed into her lover's. And then, just before she reached him, she wavered, her glance fell, went this way and that as though seeking for reassurance.

Then with a cry she fell on her knees by Poirot.

'Is this true? Is this true?'

He put both hands on her shoulders, a firm, kindly touch.

'It is true, mademoiselle.'

There was no sound then but Egg's sobs.

Sir Charles seemed suddenly to have aged. It was an old man's face, a leering satyr's face.

'God damn you,' he said.

And never, in all his acting career, had words come with such utter and compelling malignancy.

Then he turned and went out of the room.

Mr Satterthwaite half sprang up from his chair, but Poirot shook his head, his hand still gently stroking the sobbing girl.

'He'll escape,' said Mr Satterthwaite.

Poirot shook his head.

'No, he will only choose his exit. The slow one before the eyes of the world, or the quick one off stage.'

The door opened softly and someone came in. It was Oliver Manders. His usual sneering expression was gone. He looked white and unhappy.

Poirot bent over the girl.

'See, mademoiselle,' he said gently. 'Here is a friend come to take you home.'

Egg rose to her feet. She looked uncertainly towards Oliver then made a step stumblingly towards him.

'Oliver . . . Take me to Mother. Oh, take me to Mother.'

He put an arm round her and drew her towards the door.

'Yes, dear, I'll take you. Come.'

Egg's legs were trembling so that she could hardly walk. Between them Oliver and Mr Satterthwaite guided her footsteps. At the door she took a hold upon herself and threw back her head.

'I'm all right.'

Poirot made a gesture, and Oliver Manders came back into the room.

'Be very good to her,' said Poirot.

'I will, sir. She's all I care about in the world – you know that. Love for her made me bitter and cynical. But I shall be different now. I'm ready to stand by. And some day, perhaps –'

'I think so,' said Poirot. 'I think she was beginning to care for you when he came along and dazzled her. Hero worship is a real and terrible danger to the young. Some day Egg will fall in love with a friend, and build her happiness upon rock.'

He looked kindly after the young man as he left the room.

Presently Mr Satterthwaite returned.

'M. Poirot,' he said. 'You have been wonderful – absolutely wonderful.'

Agatha Christie

Poirot put on his modest look.

'It is nothing – nothing. A tragedy in three acts – and now the curtain has fallen.'

'You'll excuse me –' said Mr Satterthwaite.

'Yes, there is some point you want explained to you?'

'There is one thing I want to know.'

'Ask then.'

'Why do you sometimes speak perfectly good English and at other times not?'

Poirot laughed.

'Ah, I will explain. It is true that I can speak the exact, the idiomatic English. But, my friend, to speak the broken English is an enormous asset. It leads people to despise you. They say – a foreigner – he can't even speak English properly. It is not my policy to terrify people – instead I invite their gentle ridicule. Also I boast! An Englishman he says often, "A fellow who thinks as much of himself as that cannot be worth much." That is the English point of view. It is not at all true. And so, you see, I put people off their guard. Besides,' he added, 'it has become a habit.'

'Dear me,' said Mr Satterthwaite, 'quite the cunning of the serpent.'

He was silent for a moment or two, thinking over the case.